Outlaws #6

Flagstaff Showdown

Chet Cunningham

Thorndike Press • Waterville, Maine

Published in 2004 by arrangement with Chet Cunningham.

Thorndike Press® Large Print Western.

The tree indicium is a trademark of Thorndike Press.

The text of this Large Print edition is unabridged.
Other aspects of the book may vary from the original edition.

Set in 16 pt. Plantin by Elena Picard.

Printed in the United States on permanent paper.

Library of Congress Cataloging-in-Publication Data

Cunningham, Chet.
    Flagstaff showdown / Chet Cunningham.
        p. cm. — (Outlaws ; bk. 6)
    ISBN 0-7862-5746-6 (lg. print : hc : alk. paper)
    1. Outlaws — Fiction.   2. Arizona — Fiction.
3. Large type books.   I. Title.
PS3553.U468O93 2004
    813´.54—dc21   2003054245

Flagstaff Showdown

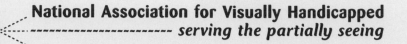

As the Founder/CEO of NAVH, the only national health agency solely devoted to those who, although not totally blind, have an eye disease which could lead to serious visual impairment, I am pleased to recognize Thorndike Press* as one of the leading publishers in the large print field.

Founded in 1954 in San Francisco to prepare large print textbooks for partially seeing children, NAVH became the pioneer and standard setting agency in the preparation of large type.

Today, those publishers who meet our standards carry the prestigious "Seal of Approval" indicating high quality large print. We are delighted that Thorndike Press is one of the publishers whose titles meet these standards. We are also pleased to recognize the significant contribution Thorndike Press is making in this important and growing field.

Lorraine H. Marchi, L.H.D.
Founder/CEO
NAVH

* Thorndike Press encompasses the following imprints: Thorndike, Wheeler, Walker and Large Print Press.

Chapter One

Mace Duncan smashed his fist into Ross Franklin's face, knocking him backward a step. Before Franklin could lift his hands, the bigger man pounded four more blows into Franklin's head, dropping him to his knees.

Mace was nearly six feet tall, heavily built with black hair and a full dark beard. His dark eyes glinted with excitement and fear as he slammed his hobnail boot into Franklin's stomach. The slightly built mill hand sagged to the floor where he doubled over, moaning in pain. Mace's second kick skidded across the side of the other man's head jolting him flat onto the wooden floor of the Johnson Lumber Mill office.

"Damn, I hate a snitch!" Mace spat. "You're a lying bastard who's a spy for Mrs. Johnson. Get up, Franklin, so you can hear me better. Come on, I didn't hurt you that bad." Mace threatened to kick the man on the floor again. Franklin looked at him in fear and disbelief, then slowly got to his knees.

"Now, you bastard, how the hell long you been spying on me?"

Franklin groaned. His hand came up to the side of his face, and he felt and then saw blood on his fingers as he pulled his hand away. Franklin looked up at the larger man looming over him. He struggled to stand, but his knee gave way, and he sat down hard on the wooden floor.

"How long, Franklin? You tell me right now or I'll kick you straight into hell!" Mace's face was red now, his squinting eyes almost shut. His breath came rapidly and sweat beaded his forehead. "How long?"

"About three months," Franklin said staring at Mace. "I worked for her long before you came here. She figures you're not reporting all the money coming in from the lumber sales."

Mace nodded. "Yeah, *she figures*, she thinks. That means that she don't have no proof. You sure as hell ain't gonna get her any proof, Franklin."

Franklin shook his head. "So you *are cheating her*. How could you do that? She's been good to you. You were a roustabout when you came here two years ago."

"Shut up, old man!"

Franklin snorted. "Always figured you changed your name and was wanted somewhere. I'm right about that, ain't I, Mace?"

"Told you to shut up!" Mace's face grew redder, he bunched his hands into fists and swung at Franklin, but the older man dodged the blow.

"She's on to you, Mace. You won't last another week."

"Bastard! You bastard!"

Mace bellowed in rage as he looked around frantically for a weapon. He grabbed the sturdy wooden chair from beside his desk. He was only a step from Franklin, who now sensed real danger. Franklin tried to get to his feet, but his knee gave away again, and he slumped on the floor.

Mace jumped toward him, screaming in fury, and slammed the heavy chair against Franklin's head with all of his strength. Franklin couldn't dodge it. One hand came up, but the chair blasted it aside; then the thick side of the chair seat hit Franklin's forehead making a curious sound. It was a little like a ripe melon splitting open.

The force of the heavy chair smashed Franklin to the floor, where he lay without moving. Both his arms were outstretched, his face bruised where it had skidded along the wooden floor.

Mace's dark eyes were furious. He dropped the chair, now feeling his lungs burning as he gulped down huge breaths of air. He shivered, then wiped sweat from his forehead with one hand. Mace stared at Franklin for a minute. Slowly his breathing settled down, and he shook his head as if to clear it.

"Franklin, you're a dirty son of a bitch, you know that?" When Franklin made no response, Mace frowned. "Come on, Franklin, I didn't hit you that hard. Get up and get out of here before I really get mad."

The man on the floor didn't move. Mace waited a minute longer, then knelt beside him. Franklin's forehead was a bloody pulp where the thick oak chair seat had struck him. His eyes stared blankly, and a little blood pooled on the floor under his head.

Mace nudged Franklin's shoulder. "Come on, Franklin, I'll get you down to Doc Warnick. We'll say you fell going down a ladder. Franklin?"

Mace touched Franklin's neck where the artery usually pulsated. He felt around a minute, then pinched Mace's nose. There was no breathing, no pulse.

"Goddamn!" Mace Duncan said softly.

10

"I killed you!" He sat back on his heels watching the body. He had to move Franklin where it would look like he had suffered an accident. Franklin usually worked a cutoff saw where the lumber was cut into eight-, ten- or twelve-foot lengths.

Mace took a deep breath and then shivered. He'd never touched a dead man before. Then he snorted. A dead man couldn't hurt him. He took another long breath, then grabbed Franklin's arm and tugged it over his shoulder and lifted the corpse to his back. He grabbed Franklin's other arm and carried him out of the office, thankful that he wasn't a heavy man.

The only other men in the mill were the Mexican saw filer and Old Charley, a man who lost a foot in a woods accident a year ago. Mace kept him on as a night watchman, mostly so the still hot steam engine wouldn't cause any problems at night by setting fire to the mill. The fire was out in the engine, but Mace had seen one saw-mill burn down because of a faulty steam engine that supplied the power to turn the big saw. Old Charley would be at the far end of the log pond about now starting his rounds. There was no chance he would see what Mace was doing. And if the Mexican saw anything, Duncan would just have to take care of him.

It took Mace ten minutes to pick the right spot. Near the cutoff saw was a wooden ladder leading down to the cleared area where the raw lumber was stacked in the sun to dry. It was only a ten-foot drop but would have to do. Mace rested Franklin on the edge of the platform near the ladder and tipped him off headfirst. The body hit with a soft, strange sound.

Mace hurried down the ladder and looked over the body. He moved Franklin a little and smashed the wounded place on his head into the two-by-four that formed the ladder. He doubled one arm under the corpse and sprawled out one leg. He checked the position, then sneaked out of the mill, making sure Old Charley did not see him.

Mace knew he had a problem. It had been a sweet deal here ever since the owner, Karl Johnson, had died and left the mill to his wife. She didn't know anything about the mill or the woods. She hired a manager, and when he hadn't worked out, she picked Mace to run the mill because he'd been there for a year and knew every job in the place.

For two months he ran it square. Then when he saw how much money could be made, he upped the work load and production and began selling all the stacks of lumber he could. The first month he pocketed over $500. Since then his take had grown larger each month.

But then that damned snoop Franklin had come nosing around and ruined everything. Maybe it was time to move on and change his name again. He had a nice little nest egg — over $50,000 in greenbacks stashed away in safe places. Not even his secretary realized that he'd hidden thousands of dollars in boxes that supposedly stored old files. He had no problem there.

Mace walked down Main Street toward the back door of the house he rented for four dollars a month. There were only about 20 frame houses in the whole town of Flagstaff, Arizona Territory, and the town only had one street.

A tattered American flag hung motionless high on a spar pole tree over the town. An enthusiastic logger had scaled the tree years earlier and nailed up the flag and named the town Flagstaff. Now whenever the flag became too worn, another logger climbed the tree and nailed up a new one. Somebody wanted to put up a rope and a pulley on top, but the townsfolk said that would violate the tradition.

The town's only link with the rest of the world was a railroad that had been built into town a year before. It was the end of the line, so far, for the Atlantic and Pacific Railroad. Dozens of tents stood just beyond the tracks on the downhill side. On the uphill slope more than a dozen frame buildings had been built, their lumber so newly sawn by the local mill that it was still pale yellow in places. Beyond these new structures were some older buildings that had turned gray from the weathering of the unpainted wood. Only two of the town's buildings were painted.

On his way home, Mace passed by a new saloon, a dance hall, Stern's General Store, a barbershop, and the town's only hotel, which was also its only two story building. The houses, such as they were, had been scattered uphill and back along the tracks.

He saw few people on the street. It was past nine in the evening, and most working folks were in bed. The saloon still roared as the woodsmen and the railroad men took turns insulting each other and then buying each other drinks.

Just past the hotel, Mace turned and walked a half a block to the small frame house he rented. He went in the back door and saw that there was at least one lamp burning in the living room, but Polly wasn't in there. He looked in the bedroom and found her sitting on the bed wearing only a flimsy nightgown.

"Where the hell you been so long?" she demanded.

He held up one finger in curt reprimand and she nodded.

"Okay, honey, I'm sorry. I just worry about you. All them dangerous machines and saws and things. Heard about a man getting sawed right in half through his belly once in a sawmill."

"Told you, Polly, you don't have to worry about me." He dropped on the bed beside her. "You just worry about taking care of my personal needs."

She squealed in delight and pulled off the thin nightgown, then began undressing him.

Less than a block down the street in the town's largest house, Harriet Johnson paced the living room floor. She looked at the chiming clock that sat on the mantle and frowned.

Franklin had promised to come that night with some evidence that she could use against Mace Duncan. Oh, she could fire the man, but she wanted to put him in the local jail and then in the territorial prison at Yuma. He deserved it. She also wanted to get back some $15,000 to $20,000 that she figured he had stolen from her. To her that much money was a fortune. Most of the men who worked in the mill earned a dollar a day in wages, six dollars a week, $24 a month.

Twenty thousand dollars would equal a hardworking man's wages for more than 57 years. She had done the mathematics with her pencil one day, and she was outraged at her discovery. He didn't put the money in the bank, which wasn't unusual. But she couldn't do anything against Duncan without evidence. The Flagstaff Bank was owned by. H. L. Rushmore, whom nobody in town trusted. And Rushmore himself told her that Duncan had no savings in the bank when she asked him.

So where did Mace hide all the money he had swindled her out of?

If her late husband were still alive, no one would have swindled him. But he'd been dead and gone now for almost a year. He died in an accident less than six months after he started the mill and furnished all of the lumber to build the town. He'd had such big plans. She had been lucky to marry him.

Harriet realized when she was a young girl that she was no beauty. Her mother told her she'd probably have to trap a man by telling him she was pregnant. Of course, in order for that ruse to work, she would have had to take some man to bed. But no boy her own age would even look at her because she was an ungainly six feet tall by the time she was 15 years old.

But then Karl had come along and bought her basket at the church picnic, and a month later they were married. During their courtship, she didn't allow him to do more than kiss her and touch her breasts once. Everyone was amazed that anyone would want to marry the clumsy girl.

That had been back in Texas. She was Texas-sized, at six foot one in her stocking feet, when she married. Karl had been almost six foot six and he took to her right away. He had married her when she was 16. He was 26.

Harriet never got past the sixth grade in book learning, but she could read well and read everything she could find. After several months of wedded life, she realized she was pregnant. She listened to her mother and took care of herself.

Having a baby was a natural thing. Animals on the farm had them all the time with no special care or fuss. At that time, Karl ran a small store one town over from her home, and her parents thought of them as well off. Nevertheless, Harriet often felt lonely and wished she didn't have to live ten miles from her parents.

When the child came she was home alone with Karl. The boy was so large that Karl had some trouble birthing him, but at last the cord was cut and her son was beside her. Karl named the child Gunner after his grandfather, and the boy grew larger than his mother.

Some folks said that Gunner was a bit slowwitted, but it wasn't true. Gunner just took his time in answering because he liked to think things through before he said a word. Even so, some folks made fun of him. Gunner never got far in school, quitting when he was 12 and larger than the man teacher.

When Gunner was 17 he ran away. He told his ma that he was tired of folks laughing at him. He wanted to go to a place where nobody knew him and earn his own way. Harriet had cried when he left, but Karl said that it would be good for him, that he'd be back in six months.

He did come back for a while, but said it

was much better where he was up in Missouri. Now and then Gunner had somebody write a letter for him to his mother, and Harriet had answered every one.

It had been almost a year since she'd heard from him. She told him in her last letter that she and Karl were moving to Flagstaff, Arizona. "If ever you get out that way," she wrote, "stop by and see us. It's not a big town, so you won't have trouble finding the Karl Johnson's place."

But as Harriet stared out the window at the darkness she wasn't thinking of her son. Where was Ross Franklin? He had promised for sure that he would be there tonight to give her the evidence about Mace Duncan. For a moment a chill passed over her. Could something have happened to Ross? No, he knew the mill better than anyone. She should have made him the manager, not Duncan. She knew that now. After Duncan was in jail, she just might ask Ross if he'd like to run the mill.

Harriet waited another hour, then carried her lamp from the living room into the bedroom and closed the door. She remembered the fine times there with Karl. But those days were over. She was 46 years old and she would not remarry. Men these days liked those spry, young girls who were only five-foot three.

There would be no more loving a good man for her. She sat on the bed and slowly undressed. As she drifted off to sleep, she was still wondering what had happened to Ross Franklin and that evidence against Mace he had promised her.

Chapter Two

The Willy Boy Gang took its time with a leisurely ride up the Rio Grande River to El Paso, where the five men rested for two days before moving north on a stage toward Albuquerque, New Mexico Territory. There they caught the Atlantic and Pacific railroad and rode in comfort along the thirty-fifth parallel toward the end of the line at Flagstaff.

It turned out to be a spectacular ride, sliding up the slopes of the Rocky Mountains on the thin rails of steel, lancing through the pass and across the continental divide, and then running downhill into Flagstaff.

"Is that the elevation?" the Professor said, staring at a small sign as the train slowed to a stop at the train-level platform. The Professor was the oldest of the Willy Boy Gang and at 25 had taught school and had even gone for over a year to Illinois College in Jacksonville. The Professor was a professional bank robber and one of the best at his trade. An expert with explosives and the smartest man in the gang, he was also a fancy dresser, a smooth talker and a lady's man.

"Flagstaff, Elevation 6910 feet," Eagle read from the sign. Eagle was a full-blooded Comanche Indian. "Don't try to run very far up here," he said. "The air is thin and you'll tire out in a hurry."

The Comanche was 18 years old. Having been raised as an Indian until the age of 12, he knew all of the Comanche skills, traditions, and ways of living. When he was 12, he was captured by the cavalry and sent to a Catholic mission school, where he had learned quickly to read and write English. At 15, he ran away from the school because the white boys ganged up on him and beat him time and time again.

Once outside the school Eagle had to steal to live and soon wound up in jail in Oak Park, Texas. It was there he met the other five members of the Willy Boy Gang.

Willy Boy, the five-foot-five-inch leader of the group, shrugged at Eagle's recommendation against running a lot. He was 18 and had killed more men than he could remember. "Hell, we won't be doing the running, but we might be chasing somebody. So remember what Eagle says."

Willy Boy had led the band of six out of the Oak Park, Texas jail after faking his own hanging in his cell. Once he was free, Willy Boy released everyone in the jail, but they did not escape without a battle; and they ended up killing two deputy sheriffs while getting away. After their escape, they had had to fight off two posses and a famous bounty hunter. Through all of their conflicts with the law, the six had forged a bond that would hold them close forever.

Now, a full year after their breakout, they had all the money they would ever need, thanks to the one member of their group who had died in San Francisco. Before he was murdered, Johnny Joe Williams had won over $350,000 in a big-stakes, winner-take-all poker game. He had banked his winnings, making Willy Boy and the Professor co-signers with him on the checking account. Soon afterwards, the angry loser of the gang had Johnny killed, and the remaining five men in the Willy Boy Gang tracked down the hired gun and the gambler who paid him and shot them dead.

It was only by accident that they learned about the money waiting for them in the bank. They were almost caught trying to get some of the money, but now could draw on it at any time by sending a notice of withdrawal to the bank by mail. The five of them had a fortune on demand and split any withdrawal they made five ways.

Just before the train came to a stop, Willy Boy spoke softly so the other people on the car couldn't hear him. "Remember, we get off one at a time, register in ones or twos at the hotel, and help Gunner anyway we can. This is his game and we play it his way."

Gunner watched the other four and nodded. They had come all this way to help him find his ma and see if she was all right. He hadn't heard from her for a year because he'd been moving around too fast with the Willy Boy Gang. Now they were actually here in Flagstaff, and he'd have a chance to find her.

Gunner was 21 years old, six-foot-four inches tall, and built as wide and as strong as a young longhorn bull. His best weapon was a double-barreled, sawed-off shotgun he carried on a cord around his neck. The young man was a born follower. In his year with the gang, he had become Willy Boy's protector and shadow. He was devoted to the younger, smaller man, and it was evident that he would die to save his leader if that was required. Now, as the train came to a halt, he grinned at the others and started for the end of the car and the door to the platform.

A line of people waited to get off, and Gunner couldn't help but grin again. He nodded when the man ahead of him turned and glanced at him.

"I'm here to see my ma," Gunner told the man. The stranger lifted his brows, mumbled something, and turned away. Behind Gunner, Willy Boy saw the exchange and patted his tall friend on the shoulder. When Gunner turned to look at Willy Boy, the leader of the pack grinned and nodded, and they moved on to the platform.

"This is a town?" the Professor grumbled as he stepped from the car to the wooden platform. There wasn't even a station building. Ahead he saw the loop siding of the rail line where the train would swing around and rejoin the main track to head back east. He wished he were taking the train back to a real city.

"Probably not even a good poker game in the whole place," the Professor growled to himself as he walked down the muddy street. It had rained all morning before the gang arrived, but the sun had broken through the clouds and shined warmly. Not paying attention to where he was going, the Professor stepped into an inch of muddy water and swore.

Willy Boy grinned as he glanced back at his friend and saw him shaking his wet pant leg. This was his kind of town. Maybe 500 or 600 people, probably not even a town marshal, and there had to be some railroad money or a payroll coming in from the east. He decided to try to work out some amusement for the gang before they left.

Hell, Gunner's mom was probably as happy as a robin on her nest, and they could get out of there in a couple of days and head on toward Sacramento. That was where a lot of the gold from the California mines wound up, and Willy Boy figured there were a few hundred pounds of gold there just waiting for him to ride in and take his share.

An hour later, all of the gang had registered in the Flagstaff hotel and wandered one at a time into room #14, Willy Boy's spot. Juan Romero, the fifth man in the gang, shook his head when he entered. "Damn near didn't let me register," he said. "The room clerk said they didn't usually take Mexicans here. I showed him three twenty-dollar gold pieces, and he let me in, but said I shouldn't try to eat in the

26

dining room. They don't like Mexicans in this town."

Willy Boy puffed on a long black cigar, as had been his habit lately. "Don't pay them no mind, Juan. Hell, you should just buy the damned hotel, and then see what they say. You can afford to do it if you want to."

The men all laughed.

"One thing's certain," Willy Boy said. "We got to hold it down here. No place to hide. Four, maybe five hundred people. We make sure not to spend too much money. We don't get in no damn trouble, and we don't cause a big disturbance. We never eat together or be seen as a bunch in public. And we stay out of trouble.

"There still might be a lawman or two looking for us, or even a tough bounty hunter. We're still worth ten thousand dollars to some bastard if he can kill us or turn us in. Nobody knows where we are, so let's keep it that way. We broke down Deputy Sheriff Seth Andrews from Oak Park, but there could be another one coming out of the woods trying to find us.

"If we decide to take the bank or a railway express car or something, we plan it out and we do it just as we leave. But first, we wait and make sure Gunner finds his Ma and that everything is fine with her. Any questions?"

Eagle, who had cut his hair and wore a hat and his regular white man's clothes, held up several pads of lined paper. "If you need me, I'll be in my room working on my next book about my people. I didn't get much done on it the last few weeks."

Willy Boy looked around.

The Professor shrugged. "I'll be looking for a poker game that is up to my high standards."

"Meaning the other guy needed to have played poker more than twice before," Willy Boy said. They all laughed again.

Gunner held up his hand. "I'd like to go and find my ma. She might have me in for supper."

The others nodded and Gunner slipped out the door, closing it behind him without making a sound. He walked down the hall to the steps and out of the hotel. At the general store, Gunner asked the man behind a small counter next to a cracker barrel if he knew Mrs. Karl Johnson.

The man nodded. "Mrs. Johnson. Yes, sir. She's an important lady in this town. Her husband died a year or so ago, and now she's the owner of the Johnson Sawmill and Lumber Company. The office is down there about a block beyond the train station. But Mrs. Johnson won't be there. She spends most all of her time at her big house, the three-story painted one with light blue trim. It's down about a block the other way."

Gunner thanked the man and hurried out. So his ma really was here and she owned the sawmill! He'd heard the screeching of the saw as they sliced through the big ponderosa pine logs. A stack belched smoke back along the tracks, and Gunner wondered just how big the mill was. When he'd walked another few yards, he could see the three-storied house on the corner of the next street. It was the only house on that block, and it was huge!

Gunner walked faster as he came closer to the house. Then he ran the last 20 feet to the gate in the middle of the white picket fence that surrounded the lot. He fumbled with the latch on the gate, finally got it open, then hurried up the walk to the front door.

Gunner looked at the black metal button on the door, ignored it, and knocked sharply with his knuckles on the painted wood. The big man shifted his weight from one foot to the other. His trail-smudged gray hat rested in his hands, where he turned it around an inch at a time.

He frowned and was about to reach up to knock again when he heard footsteps inside, and then the door swung open.

"Ma!" Gunner said.

Harriet Johnson's eyes went wide with surprise; then tears gushed as she caught Gunner in her long arms and crushed him to her chest. "My little boy! Oh, my little boy has come home!" She cried for two minutes, then tugged him inside and closed the door. She wiped the wetness from her eyes and stood back.

"Gunner, you're looking thin. Have you been eating properly?"

They both laughed. It was the way she always greeted him when he came home. They went into the living room, and for a half hour Gunner told her what had happened since he had last written her when he was in jail in Texas. Even though he neglected to mention some of the shoot-outs, Gunner figured he had told his mother too much.

"You can't stay with those man any longer," Harriet Johnson told Gunner. "I've got the mill now, and I need you to help me run it. There are a lot of things you can do. Why just yesterday one of the men who was helping me so much fell and was killed in the mill. Now I don't know where to turn."

"The Professor could help you, Ma. He's smart and taught school and went to college and everything."

"Oh, my goodness, I wouldn't think of it. You said this Professor actually robbed banks."

"That was just because he had to," Gunner said, stammering a little. "He ain't robbed anything now in — well, not for a lot of months. Why don't I ask him to supper tonight? Then you could tell him all about your problems at the mill?"

"If I do that, will you promise to stay home with me here in Flagstaff and help me? Nobody will laugh at you in Flagstaff, not while I own the mill and employ most of the workers in town."

Gunner rubbed his forehead as he sometimes did when a new idea tried to break into his mind. He frowned. "I don't know, Ma. I have to think on it before I promise I will. Now, can I bring the Professor for supper?"

Mrs. Johnson smiled and nodded. She had never been able to deny her only child anything.

It took Gunner almost an hour to find the Professor. Eagle was in his room writing on his book, Juan had taken a walk into the forest, and Willy Boy was talking with one of the whores in the Undercut Saloon. None of them had seen the Professor. It turned out that the Professor had taken a long bath at the hotel, then settled into a late afternoon poker game at the Logger's Rest Saloon.

He bet $20 against the last man in the hand and bluffed through his win scraping in almost $75 in the pot. He had seen Gunner come in and now looked at him. The Professor asked to sit out a hand while he went to the privy. Then he met Gunner outside the back door of the saloon.

Gunner grinned at his friend. "Figured you got my signal, Professor."

The Professor listened to Gunner's plea. The bank robber pushed his black, wide-brimmed hat back on his head and scowled. "You're telling me your ma is having problems at the mill. Then this gent who was trying to help her winds up dead after a fall of ten feet? Sounds more like he'd get a broken arm and leg, not a smashed-in skull." The Professor snorted and ran a finger around the inside of his tight white starched shirt collar.

"Hell, yes, little friend. Tell your ma I'll be glad to come and have supper with her at six tonight. The three-story house with the blue trim. I won't forget."

Gunner grinned and waved and walked out the alley and back to Main Street, where he stopped at the general store to buy his mother a present. He walked around the store for a half hour and still didn't buy anything. He didn't have the slightest idea what to get for her. At last the store owner came up and smiled and asked if he could offer some suggestions.

Chapter Three

Bert Filmore stared hard at the railroad clerk in Albuquerque, New Mexico Territory. The small man behind the grill lifted his eyes in despair.

"Young man, I sell tickets to maybe a hundred people a day. How do you expect me to remember who I sold tickets to a week ago?"

"I expect you to because you're a smart man who has a good memory for faces. How many tickets do you sell to Indians? How many tickets to a single Mexican man traveling alone? But what about a man who is six-foot-four inches and maybe a little slow? Those three you would remember."

The clerk sighed. He had been talking with this intense young man for an hour whenever there wasn't a customer at the window. Now he looked at the big railroad clock on the wall. It was against policy to talk about ticket buyers. This young man didn't even have a warrant and he certainly wasn't a lawman.

"All right, just to get rid of you. I remember the three men you mention, and they were here three or four days ago. I sold most of the tickets that morning for the eastbound train, and I had to redo the tickets westbound for two of them. A natural mistake. The Indian was polite as could be, spoke perfect English, knew more big words that I do. He even had his hair cut white man's style and wore regular clothes. I knew he was Indian, though because of his dark skin. It isn't red at all, did you know that?"

"Yes, I knew that. Where did they go?"

"The three of them all got tickets to the end of the line. Fact is, all the tickets I sold that day were going all the way to Flagstaff. I've never been there. On my next vacation I'm going out there on my pass to see what that country is like."

Bert Filmore thanked the clerk and bought a ticket to Flagstaff. The clerk assured him that the afternoon train would be on time and that it would be in the station in about an hour.

Bert sat on a wooden bench. It gave him some time to catch up. Ever since he turned 19, he had wanted to get on the trail of the Willy Boy Gang. Then when Deputy Sheriff Seth Andrews came back from Denver, Bert had talked to him for hours.

Seth was a broken man. He was still a deputy, but he had lost his anger, lost all desire to try to capture the Willy Boy Gang.

"I should have had them at Denver. I figured it had to be that one bank. But they never arrived. I waited for three days with two policemen, then the vice-president of the bank came out and told me that Mr. Thadius had been in the bank two days before and closed his account."

Evidently that had been the final blow that crushed Deputy Andrews. He said he'd never chase the Willy Boy Gang again. Bert kept Andrews talking about them, about the times he had been close, the two times when the gang could have killed him, but let him ride out.

After talking for two hours, Deputy Andrews suddenly frowned. "Oh, no, Bert. Not you. You're not going to try to find the Willy Boy Gang are you?"

"Damn straight I am. They killed my Pa same night they shot you, Deputy Andrews. I tried to get the sheriff to make me a deputy, but he said I had to be twenty-one, and that's too long to wait. I'm going on my own. The wanted poster is still out on them, so there's a ten-thousand-dollar reward for all five.

"Mr. Chambers at the general store said he'd stake me with a trail outfit and enough cash for the hunt. If I find them, he gets half of the reward. He's a cousin of my Pa. I'm going just as soon as I can talk some more to you."

"You'll get yourself killed, boy."

"Maybe, but that works both ways. I need to get some revenge, Deputy. I need to shoot down one of them bastards to even up the score for Pa. It's what he would have wanted me to do. So the more you can tell me about them, the better off I'll be. Didn't you send back some reports?"

They dug out the reports, and Deputy Andrews turned over his notebook to Bert. In it he had descriptions and paragraphs about each of the five outlaws. Bert studied everything, read it over again and again until he knew as much about the men as he could without actually seeing them.

Deputy Andrews had one last talk with Bert before he left that day almost a month ago.

"My guess," he told Bert, "is that they went to Mexico or to the Rio Grande somewhere to find the Mexican's people. Looks like they've been trying to help each of the men in the gang to take care of some unfinished business or find kinfolk, that sort of thing. With Eagle it was revenge against the army unit that massacred his family.

"The Professor went back to the bank and he almost got killed, but they still managed to clean out all the cash. Now I don't know what they might do, but Juan Romero and the tall guy, Gunner Johnson, are the two that haven't had any help from the gang yet. My guess is Juan. Best thing you can do is head down to the Rio Grande and ask some questions.

"Oh, check with county sheriffs along the way to watch for a string of bank robberies." Seth Andrews paused. "Course, now that they have all that gambling money from Johnny Joe Williams, they probably won't be hitting as many banks as they did." For ten minutes he explained again the gang's technique going into a bank just at closing time and rarely firing a shot during a robbery.

Bert shifted on the hard bench as he waited for the train. He had gone to the

Rio Grande. He had stopped in San Antonio first, but could find nothing about a gang of five men with one Indian, a Mexican, and a giant in the mixture.

He headed due south to Laredo, but picked up no information about the five men. Slowly he worked west along the muddy flow of the mighty Rio Grande. He arrived at Eagle Pass, Texas, on the river a week after the gang had been there. He had gone across the river to Piedras Negras and talked to some of the people. Yes, Juan Romero had been there, and he was a saint. He had taken down the *federales* captain and routed his men and returned to the people thousands of American dollars that had been stolen from them over the years.

It didn't make sense. He learned that Juan's son had been murdered and that his wife had died after being sold into prostitution. It made even less sense then that Juan would give the money he and the others had taken from the *federales* to the villagers. Bert was hunting a band of ruthless killers, but the people of this small village called them saints.

Now the trail was warmer, but still he had lost time. They had ridden out of Eagle Pass and moved up to the El Paso trail. From there it had been easy to identify them as the five men who caught a stage and then the railroad north.

He was still three days behind them, but at least he had them pinned down in Flagstaff. There was only a rough stage road west from there, the California Trail.

Flagstaff — the place sounded like the end of the world. Why would a band of killers go there? That made Bert think about what Deputy Andrews had told him about the gang. Andrews said when they went to some small town or state, it seemed that they had a specific purpose for going there. In Missouri they looked for the killer who had shot down Willy Boy's father. In Idaho they had helped Eagle find the man who had been in on the killing of his parents when the cavalry raided his Comanche village. They made the trip to San Francisco so Johnny Joe Williams could play his dream game of poker with the big boys. Then they went to Denver so the Professor could rob that same bank again. And the Mexico trip was to reunite Juan Romero with his wife and son.

But why were they going to Flagstaff? The only one left who hadn't had a trip of his own was the big slow-witted man, Gunner Johnson. No, Deputy Andrews said that Gunner was not feeble-minded. He was simply a little slow sometimes in talking and reasoning, but his trigger finger was lightning fast.

Flagstaff? Gunner Johnson? The train pulled into the Albuquerque station right on time and left three minutes later. The station agent said if nothing went wrong the train would pull into Flagstaff sometime the next morning.

As he rode along on the shiny steel rails, Bert Filmore remembered his father and the good times they used to have, remembered the night that he died and the terrible days that followed. Now at long last, he was about to have a chance to pay back the outlaws who had ended his father's life. At last!

Bert watched the land slant past out the window, and knew he was traveling as fast as anyone in the world could. But he wanted the train to go faster. Why couldn't it go 1000 miles in an hour? That way he would be in Flagstaff within minutes. He cupped his chin with his hand and stared out the window. For a moment it seemed like tomorrow would never come.

When Gunner went back to his mother's house from the general store, he carried a package carefully wrapped in brown paper by the store owner. He knocked on the door, and when his mother came, she hugged him again before they went inside.

"It's so good to have you home, Gunner. I'm hoping that you'll want to stay here with me now. I need a man around the place to take care of things. Besides, there are two or three jobs at the mill I want you to do for me."

Gunner looked confused for a minute, nodded, then handed his mother the package.

"A present for you, your birthday present. I missed it again."

"Now, Gunner. You know I don't hold with celebrations just because of a birthday. But, since you went to all the trouble —" Her face betrayed emotions countering her words, and she smiled as she unwrapped the box. Inside swathed in white tissue paper was a heavy brown and white glass vase. It had two places for flowers and two handles. Mrs. Johnson loved it at once.

"Gunner, how did you know I was short on vases? I have so many flowers and not enough vases for them. Let me go out and get some roses right now and put them in some water. It's just what I needed."

Gunner grinned and wandered around the big house until his mother came back. He stopped in the kitchen and lifted a lid on a pot on the stove. It looked like stew. He sniffed and his mother came in.

"Caught you checking out my cooking," Harriet Johnson said. "Just like old times in Texas. Now, tell me how these men you're riding with are treating you?"

As he told her about the Professor and how he was so smart and helped everyone, Mrs. Johnson worked around the kitchen. She had a chicken on the stove steaming in a covered fry pan that she had browned to a turn earlier. The stew contained four kinds of vegetables and chunks of chicken.

She turned and smiled as she watched Gunner. "I can't tell you how good it is to have you home, young man," she said. "Just so good. I'm hoping you'll want to stay." She frowned a moment, then smiled when he looked up.

"I did invite a special guest for dinner. This is a wonderful person I think you'll like. Now, you best get your hands washed, it's getting on toward six o clock and our guests will be coming any minute."

The Professor arrived promptly at six, and both Gunner and his mother met him. The Professor took Mrs. Johnson's hand

and kissed the back of it and smiled.

"Well now, I'm mighty pleased to meet you, Mrs. Johnson. Gunner gets on a talking streak now and again, and he's told us a lot about his family."

Mrs. Johnson had never had a man kiss her hand before. She stared in wonder at the Professor a moment, then nodded and nearly blushed. "Yes, I see. It's good to meet one of Gunner's friends. Now come in, supper is almost ready. We have to wait for one more guest before we sit down."

They waited in the parlor, and the Professor saw at once that Mrs. Johnson had spent a lot of her sawmill money furnishing the house. She had bought good furniture, undoubtedly brought in by train from somewhere in the east. The matching sofa and overstuffed chairs had sleek cherry wood legs and backs. A piano sat to one side of the parlor, and the cover was open as if it were played often. A deep woven oriental rug covered most of the hardwood floor, and the room was dusted, spotless.

Before Mrs. Johnson could get to the problem at the mill, the doorbell rang, and the lady of the house came back a moment later with the last guest. She was about 25, tall and thin with wary blue eyes and soft brown hair that came below her shoulders. She wore a Sunday-Go-To-Meeting dress of pale green that clashed with her eyes.

"Everyone, I'd like you to meet Effy Hendricks," Mrs. Johnson said. "Effy is my neighbor and one of my dear friends. She's starting a library here in Flagstaff."

Effy hesitated, then a brief smile broke her frozen face for a moment, and she nodded to each of the men in turn. Her hands held a crumpled linen handkerchief which she twisted first one way and then the other.

The Professor held out his hand and grasped hers for a moment. "I'm pleased to meet you, Effy," he said and let go of her hand.

Gunner stood there, his eyes wide, his own face a mask of surprise and irritation.

Mrs. Johnson scowled at her son. "Gunner, say hello to Effy. I've told her a lot about you."

Gunner nodded and took a step backward. Mrs. Johnson sighed and caught Effy's hand. "Don't worry, dear, Gunner has always been shy around people he doesn't know. Now, it's time to eat. Shall we go into the dining room."

She and Effy led the way. The Professor gave Gunner an amused look. He was sure the old woman had brought Effy to dinner with the hopes of interesting Gunner in her. Effy was a bit strange, but then so was Gunner; they just might hit it off.

The Professor made sure he was in place to help Mrs. Johnson sit down. Gunner stayed half a room away from Effy and quickly sat down when the others did.

When the Professor saw there was a salad on the plates for each person, he smiled at Mrs. Johnson. "I bet you have your own garden, Mrs. Johnson. There isn't a place in town you could find this many greens for a salad."

Harriet Johnson smiled. "Why, yes, I do have a garden. In fact Effy and I work in it almost every day. You'll be surprised when we show it to you. Effy is so good with growing things." She looked sharply at Gunner, but he was busy sampling the salad. He nibbled on a long green onion, put it down, then had a bite of the lettuce before putting down his fork.

A minute later Mrs. Johnson left the room and returned with the main course and side dishes. She had made golden-brown fried chicken and chicken stew that had thickened gloriously into a chicken gravy, with six kinds of vegetables instead of four, and tall glasses of ice-cold lemonade.

"Here in Flagstaff we have no shortage of ice," Mrs. Johnson said. "We have a city ice pond, and each winter the men cut the frozen slabs and haul them to the ice house. They put down straw and then put straw between the chunks. The ice always lasts through the whole summer."

Most of the dinner talk was between Mrs. Johnson and the Professor. She inquired about his college and how he liked it. Twice his mother asked Gunner questions, but received only one word answers. Gunner looked at Effy now and then, but everytime he found her looking at him he darted his glance away from her.

Effy didn't say a word during the whole meal. Mrs. Johnson served bread pudding for dessert and then urged the three guests into the parlor while she cleaned up the table. Effy went cautiously, glaring at her shoes the whole way out. She sat down on the sofa, but as soon as the men sat down, she mumbled something, rose, and hurried to the kitchen.

There were voices in the kitchen for a moment, then the back door closed. A minute later Harriet Johnson came into the parlor wiping her hands on her apron.

"I declare, I don't know what to think of young folks these days. Effy said she had to hurry home and check on her sick cat. The poor dear was frightened right out of her wits by you two handsome men. Effy never has had much to do with men. I don't think a man has ever been courting at her little house." She looked pointedly at Gunner, but he was examining his finger-nails and didn't see the glance.

The Professor moved into the conversational void smoothly. "Gunner told me that you're having some problems at your sawmill, Mrs. Johnson."

She took one more pointed look at her son, then turned toward the Professor and nodded.

"I certainly am. I'm afraid my manager is stealing money from the company, and I'm not sure what to do. My friend Ross Franklin was trying to get evidence so we could send the sheriff after Mace Duncan, but he died just yesterday. Fell off his saw rig and hit his head."

"Terribly convenient for this Mace Duncan," the Professor said.

Mrs. Johnson looked up, startled. "Convenient? You don't mean that —" She put her hand to her forehead. "Oh, dear. You can't be suggesting that Mr. Duncan had some hand in the accident that took Ross's life?"

"I'm not suggesting that, but until I find out otherwise, it would seem like a strong possibility. A man who steals a lot of money might also be capable of murder. What did the sheriff say?"

"Oh, we don't have a sheriff here in Flagstaff. Not even a town marshal just yet. There is a sheriff down in Prescott, I hear, but he don't get up here much."

"Mrs. Johnson, looks like you need a helping hand. I'll be glad to look into the problem. I'm free of any commitments right now. That is if you want my help?"

"Oh, yes, I'm at the end of my wits, but I don't know what to do."

"You'll have to tell me why you suspect him, maybe show me the books of the company, any evidence you might have."

"Yes, I'll be glad to do that. We can go down to the company office tomorrow. I'll introduce you to my nephew from Texas who's here to help me run the mill. That should work."

They talked for a few minutes more, and then the Professor stood to leave.

"Gunner, you'll be staying here, of course," his mother said. "I've got a room all ready for you."

Gunner looked stunned for a moment, then he nodded. "Yes, Ma. I'll go along to the hotel and get my gear."

On the way back to the hotel, the Professor watched Gunner.

"Hey, big guy, I like your ma. What did you think of Effy?"

"Dunno. Didn't notice her."

"I think your ma invited her so you could meet her. Effy seemed nice to me. Shy, but a lady."

"She had blue eyes," Gunner said.

The Professor grinned. "Thought you said you didn't notice her."

Gunner frowned at the Professor. "I saw her. She isn't too pretty. She's tall and skinny and she was flat in front."

The Professor laughed. "I guess you did notice her pretty well, Gunner." They had been in town less than six hours and already Gunner's mother was matchmaking. Who knew, it just might work.

Chapter Four

The next morning, the Professor met Mrs. Johnson in the hotel lobby as they had arranged, and they walked the long block to the Johnson Sawmill and Lumber Company office.

Mrs. Johnson wore a dark blue dress with a short jacket and a small blue hat and looked almost businesslike. She was tall and imposing, sturdy and not a pretty woman.

"I hope I'm doing the right thing," she said.

"If that Mr. Franklin did not die accidentally, you have a serious situation, and you and Gunner could both be in danger. I'll see what I can find out and then have a long talk with this Mace Duncan. I play some poker, so it's my business to judge a man quickly by what he does and says. Leave it up to me. If we do run into trouble, I have three other friends who will be more than glad to help. We came here on Gunner's behalf, so anything we can do, we will."

She glanced up and smiled at him, confident that he would help her. Gunner didn't accompany them to the mill that morning because he wanted to walk around town to get to know the place better. But that was just as well, for the Professor and Mrs. Johnson had worked up a plan to try to find some evidence of Mace Duncan's wrongdoing.

The Johnson sawmill sat on a cleared space not more than 50 yards from the Atlantic and Pacific rails and was a large setup. The logs came down the timbered slopes and were brought to the millpond by drag mules or on low-slung sturdy sets of logging wheels.

The men who built the sawmill had dammed up a small creek to form a log pond about 100 feet long. The logs were pushed into the pond, then maneuvered up to a chute where a cable hooked on to them and pulled them up an incline and onto the saw carriage.

The Professor and Mrs. Johnson walked past the mill itself to another building just behind it that had a sign over the door indicating it was the Johnson mill office. The building was one story, maybe 30 feet square with a small porch on the front. The Professor pulled open a screen door and let its spring pull it closed after they stepped inside. They were in a large room with four desks and a closed section in back that appeared to hold two smaller closed-off spaces. A woman working at the first desk looked up and saw them. She quickly came forward and shook Mrs. Johnson's hand.

"So good to see you down here again," the woman said. She was in her forties, and wore her dark hair pulled into a knot at the back of her head. From the open ledgers on her desk, the Professor could tell she had been working on some of the company books.

"Nancy, it's good to be here. This is my nephew from Michigan who may want to invest some of his inheritance in the company, so he'll want to check over everything. Please show him anything he wants to see and answer any questions. Is Mace here?"

The lady smiled and nodded. "Yes, shall I tell him you want to see him?"

"No, we'll go back unannounced."

She and the Professor walked between desks where one other woman and two young men worked and came to the first office door. Mrs. Johnson took the door knob and thrust the panel open. Inside was an office with a desk and some boxes in one corner and a tall, heavily built man with dark hair and a full black beard behind the desk staring out the window at the mill. He turned abruptly, his brows raising in surprise. He stood at once.

"Mrs. Johnson! I had no idea you were here."

"We just now arrived, Mr. Duncan. I'd like you to meet my nephew, Nate Brown. He's here from Michigan and may want to invest in the business and help me run it. That means he'll want to go over everything with a jaundiced eye before he puts any money into the venture."

For a moment, Duncan's eyes widened and his lips parted in surprise. But he recovered at once. "Of course, we could always use some new capital. I'll be glad to show him everything. Should we start in the woods and then go to the haul roads and the pond and the mill and finish up with the office?"

"Actually, I'd like to do it the other way around," the Professor said. "All that outside isn't worth a nickel if things go haywire in the office. I come from a long line of businessmen, Mr. Duncan. I know how a firm should be run, and this mill to me right now is just another business."

Mrs. Johnson caught Duncan's attention. "Nate told me he was surprised at the low profit we've made in the last two months. He says that with an investment of this size and a firm doing this much business the profit should be much higher."

Duncan lifted up his arms. "The gods willing, I'd also like to see a better profit picture. We're working on it."

"That's exactly what I'm going to find out. It should take me about two days to go over the books for the entire operation. Do you have any suggestions where I should start, Mr. Duncan?"

Duncan got up and walked to the window, then back to his desk. He shook his head. "No. I don't think so. One man's methods are not another's. I'd probably not start you out the way you usually work in this type of situation."

"Good," the Professor said. "Then I'd say we understand each other. I'm not an adversary, Mr. Duncan. I want you to be certain of that. I'm simply looking at the business practices and trying to see if I can offer Aunt Harriet any suggestions, as well as thinking about investing. I really want to come west, you see."

After Duncan nodded his understanding, the Professor and Mrs. Johnson went back to the main part of the office building.

"Well, he seems pleasant enough, Aunt Harriet," the Professor said. "I think I'll start with the income ledger and the accounts receivable. That's always a good place to start."

She smiled. "I'll leave you alone. I really don't understand all of this business talk. I do need to go help Effy at the new library. We're proud of our start. Already we have over five hundred books!" She touched his shoulder and talked a moment with Nancy before going out the front door.

When Mrs. Johnson departed, Professor went to Nancy's desk, and she quickly produced the two ledgers he wanted to start with. She had a desk set up for him with half-a-dozen sharpened pencils, a tablet of paper, and some white paper with the Johnson letterhead on it.

The Professor had been bluffing with a pair of sixes when he talked to Duncan about how much he knew about the business world. But it was plain that Mrs. Johnson knew nothing about business at all, which sounded like real trouble. Duncan could be hiding half the income from her and showing her reports of far less profit than the firm was making.

But for what little the Professor knew, he knew that lumbering was a good business in the west. Every new town needed wagon loads of lumber to put up its first frame buildings, and sawmills were few.

Upon examining the income ledger, he discovered it was clean, no erasures or crossed-out figures. The totals seemed to tally, but the income for the previous month was maybe one quarter of what he guessed it should be. He asked Nancy for their current price list for lumber in the various forms, two-by-fours, two-by-twelves, shiplap, one-by-sixes, and the other heavier beams and timbers.

Then he asked her for the daily production figures, the approximate board feet of lumber they sawed into lumber a day, which he used to work out an average price per board foot of the total output. According to the production figures the mill worked six days a week and produced as much lumber in a week as the books reported sold in a month. If that were true, there must be a large lot full of sawn lumber somewhere. The Professor asked Nancy if she knew of any excess lumber, but she shook her head.

"No, we seem to be selling just about as much as we're cutting. We try to let it sun dry for a while in the yard, but more often than not we ship it out still green on the train back into New Mexico and some even to northern Texas."

He thanked Nancy and went back to the books. He made a list of those firms that had bought lumber. The only way to confirm how much they were buying would be to wire them to doublecheck. That way he could also find out the total amount of their payments for the past three months. He'd do that, but he figured the key to the whole thing might be the incoming mail.

"Nancy, who handles the mail everyday?" the Professor asked.

"Oh, Mr. Duncan does that. We had a man who took care of it, but Mr. Duncan caught him cheating and he had to fire the man. Mr. Duncan works so hard. He's here late at night two or three times a week. I worry about him."

The Professor was starting to worry about him, too. "Has the mail arrived yet from the morning train?"

"No. We send Vincent up to the train. The rail clerks sort out our mail into one bag, and he picks it up straight from the railway mailman. Makes it easier on Mr. Partridge that way. He's the postmaster at the Partridge General Store."

"That's good planning. Nancy, when Vincent brings in the mail this morning, have him leave it at your desk. I want to go over it before Mr. Duncan gets it. Mrs. Johnson said for you to do whatever I asked, right?"

"Yes, of course, Mr. Brown. Mr. Duncan usually doesn't get to it until the afternoon anyway. At least that's when he brings out the checks for me to record in the income ledger."

"You record the income checks?"

"Yes, sir, every one that one comes in. Doesn't seem like we get as many as we used to."

The Professor nodded, thanked her, and went back to his figures. There had to be two sets of books — one with the real income that Duncan kept and another with the mill's income after Duncan stole his share that Nancy kept. But even if there were two sets of books, the Professor couldn't figure out how Duncan cashed the checks. Someone at the bank had to be in on it.

The bank in town wasn't much. He'd looked it over carefully the day before. There was only one teller and another man who sat at the back and a woman who worked as an accountant. Still, he'd look into it.

When he finished with the books, the Professor told Nancy he wanted to go look at the place where the accident happened. She blinked and wiped away a tear as she told him where the cutoff saw was situated. "Poor man," Nancy said. "He was so kind and good to all of us. I'm sure he was Mrs. Johnson's favorite. But now he's gone."

The Professor nodded and went out the front door. He oriented himself and found the cutoff saw platform with no trouble. Nobody seemed to pay any attention to him. He climbed the ladder to the roost where the cutoff saw evened up the lengths of the timbers into conventional sizes. The man running the saw scowled at him, turned off his rig, and came over.

"Who the hell are you?" the big man asked.

"Nate Brown, I'm related to Mrs. Johnson. Just looking around."

"Mace say you could?"

"Of course. Mrs. Johnson told him I had a free rein to see anything I wanted to. Is this where Ross Franklin fell the other night?"

The man pulled back a little. His bold stare eased and he nodded. "Yeah, dumb bastard. Guess he was getting too old to

60

work up here. Never catch me falling off, for damn sure."

"He went right down this ladder?"

"Head first, they think. Gouged half his skull off on that two-by-four down there when he hit. His head wasn't pretty. I got here before they moved him."

"Not much of a fall," the Professor said.

"Hell, don't take much when you hit your head. I got slammed by a board once on the green chain. Damn near tore my head off, and I was just standing there."

"Yeah, guess so, thanks." The Professor waved and climbed back down the ladder. He could see now where there were still dark red stains on one side of the ladder. It looked like Franklin hadn't hit his head until he got to the bottom of the ladder. It was straight up and down without any slant to it. The Professor wondered why Franklin hit so low. It was almost as if when he fell he had caught the rungs with his legs and swung his head back toward the ladder. The Professor found that very strange.

Another thought came to him. Franklin was trying to find evidence that Mrs. Johnson could take to court. What if he found it and Duncan confronted him and bashed in his head with a handy two by four? There were boards and sticks all over the place. Duncan could have carried the dead man to the ladder, crumpled him against it, maybe even slammed his head into it to make it look as if he had fallen.

Yes, that was very possible. But the Professor had to deal in facts. That's what he needed to rout Duncan and get back any cash he had been siphoning off. He was convinced that somebody was stealing cash out of the receipts because they showed only about a quarter of what the real income was. But where had the money gone?

He walked around the mill and talked with the workers. They all seemed to be pleasant, honest, hard-working men trying to make a living. Any skullduggery would have to be at the top — either Duncan, this Vincent who brought the mail sack, or someone else. It also had to involve someone at the bank. So the Professor had some leads to work on.

He decided to go to the coroner next, or whoever did the job here in Flagstaff. He stopped in the office to ask Nancy.

"On any accidental or suspicious death old Doc Marston looks over the situation. He's some kind of assistant coroner or something." Nancy frowned. "You want to talk to him about Mr. Franklin?"

"I think I should."

Nancy frowned. "Didn't seem reasonable that Ross would fall off that rig he'd worked on for two years. Doc has his office just the other side of the hotel, can't miss it. He lives upstairs."

Five minutes later, the Professor walked into the doctor's office and found the medic hard at work playing himself a game of chess. He looked up and motioned to the blacks, and the Professor sat down and checked over the board. The blacks were far ahead. He made six moves and the game ended with the white king checkmated.

"Be damned, I didn't see that coming," the doctor said.

"Play six moves ahead, Doctor, that way you can always win. The problem is trying to figure out six moves ahead." He held out his hand. "I'm known around here as Nate Brown. Mrs. Johnson tells me one of her employees died a night or so ago."

The doctor shook his hand and frowned. "Welcome to Flagstaff, Mr. Brown. I worried over that one. Finally had to put down accidental death, I couldn't see anything else. Never seen a skull smashed in that way before. The blood on the two-by-four was on the corner, but looked like the fracture was a sturdy two inches wide and flat, not a groove like the edge of a two-by-four would make. Still I didn't have anything to go on."

"Doc Marston, Ross was murdered, sure as hell. Probably never be able to prove it, but I'm glad you said what you did. Don't noise it about, but there seems to be a problem over at the mill."

"We don't need no more problems, Brown. Hard enough keeping this scallywag of a town alive as it is. If the mill closes we're in major trouble. I heard the railroad only came this far to get the timber out."

The doctor stretched out his legs, crossed his ankles, and took a long breath. He was short and on the chunky side with white hair, spectacles, and a slightly reddish nose.

"Damn, Ross. Never believed that he'd fall off that rig of his. Leastwise not and kill himself. Must have been clubbed by something, but not a two-by-four; the injury was too damn narrow. Something else did it and seems like there was a curve to it."

"The wound showed a curve?"

"Yep, peered to have a curve up and then a curve down, but the other side was

64

straight as a lead pencil. Damned if I could figure it out. But hell, I ain't supposed to be no damn detective."

He looked at the Professor. "Yeah, I guess that's your job, right?"

"Not in any way, Doctor Marston. I'm just a friend of the Widow Johnson trying to help her out a bit. Oh, you must know the banker. Is he honest? Most bankers in most small towns turn out to be rats in rabbit skins."

The doctor chuckled. "Hal Rushmore can't be a rat; he doesn't have the balls for it. He came to town with a thousand dollars and set himself up in the banking business. Now he's almost legitimate. Registered and everything. Still I don't keep much money with him. Course, I ain't got that much."

"Who works for him?"

"One clerk and a bookkeeper. Clerk is young, maybe twenty-five. Drifted in one day on the train, stayed. Guess he had banking work down the tracks somewhere."

The Professor stood. "Doc, I guess that about takes care of my aches and pains. Mark the office visit on my tab. I best be moving on."

The doctor squinted as he looked up at the Professor. "Yep, a detective if I ever seen one. You do good and watch your back. One man gets killed, likely there could be more candidates for boot hill."

"I'll remember that, Doc." The Professor waved and walked out to the street. He looked one way and saw two men suddenly take interest in a store window. The Professor frowned. He wasn't sure, but now that he eyed them, he thought he had seen the same two men when he went into Doc's office. He'd been in town less than a day so why would anyone be tracking him?

It wouldn't hurt to check them out. The Professor turned and walked directly toward the men who were about 30 feet away. One saw him coming and sauntered across the half-dried street. The second man moved ahead of the Professor down the boardwalk. The Professor walked faster and soon overtook the watcher. The Professor tapped him on the shoulder, and the man looked over at him.

"Hi, I'm looking for a match. Fresh out and I need a smoke. Could you lend me a match?"

The man shook his head, ducked, and walked directly across the street. The Professor shrugged and went up two more doors into the Partridge General Store. As soon as he got inside he looked out the window. The matchless man had stopped on the far side of the street beside the other man who had been by the first store window. Now both of them stared at the general store.

"I'll be damned!" the Professor said.

Chapter Five

Gunner walked along Main Street looking into each store. Most of them he strolled inside and checked around. At the Partridge General Store he bought a new pocket knife since he'd lost his folding knife in Texas. He also bought a fine-grain whetstone and sat on the bench in front of the store sharpening the knife.

Far down the street he saw a woman. He squinted his eyes almost shut for a moment, then shivered. The woman was Effy Hendricks, the one his mother had invited to dinner the night before. For just a moment, Gunner wanted to run up the street away from her.

Then he continued sharpening his knife. He finished the long blade and took out the shorter, heavier one and sharpened it. When he looked south down the street again, Effy was gone.

Gunner grinned, wiped the stone dust off his blade and folded the knife before putting it in his pocket. Continuing his tour of the town, he kept on going south. At the saddle shop, he watched the saddle-maker working. Then he moved on past a small café and the hotel. He thought the office next to the hotel might be the library, but saw it was a newspaper office. He was surprised for a minute because he didn't even know the town had a newspaper.

A small stitchery shop came next, and beyond that he saw a store front that seemed to be vacant. It was the one on the corner of Ponderosa Street, which crossed Main. When he looked closer he saw a small sign on the window that read, "Flagstaff Public Library." Another sign said, "Book donations gladly accepted."

He started to reach for the knob, then shivered again and looked away. He started to go by, but suddenly turned and pushed open the door. Gunner couldn't explain to himself why he did it. Something nudged him and he walked inside.

It was mostly a bare room with bookshelves along one side. Someone sat at a makeshift desk at the near wall. He looked at the woman and froze. Effy sat there smiling at him.

"Well, Gunner. I'm glad you've come to

see our library. Your mother has given us almost half of our books." She rose and he saw she wore a pretty blue-and-white dress, and at once he noticed she wasn't as flat in front as he had thought.

"Please, Gunner," Effy said and smiled, "stay a minute. I want to apologize for last night. I felt out of place and a little scared. Your ma has talked a lot about you, but I never expected to meet you. I almost didn't go, but your ma is such a good friend I just had to."

Gunner nodded, looked at her for a moment, and then shifted his glance to the books. She wasn't flat in front at all!

"I don't read much," Gunner said.

"Nobody reads much in this town. Most of the people are too busy trying to make a living. But the day will come when we'll have lots of folks coming in and checking out books."

Gunner started to tell her that he didn't know how to read, but shook his head and walked to the shelves. Some of the books had fancy covers on them, while others were just plain black or blue or green. They all had printing on them, but he didn't know what they said.

As he looked around, Effy stood beside him, talking. "Is there any particular kind of book you're interested in, Gunner? I like the novels. We have some of the good English novelists in now. My favorite is Charles Dickens. We have on the shelves *The Pickwick Papers, Oliver Twist,* and *Nicholas Nickleby.* So far I've read only the first one, but I'm working on *Oliver Twist* now. Do you like the English novelists?"

"Don't know," Gunner stammered. He shouldn't have stopped in the library! He desperately wanted to get out of there. How could he do it without making her feel bad? But why should he care how she felt?

"I was about to make some coffee, Gunner. There's a small apartment in the back of the library where I live. Would you like to have some coffee with me? I have some fresh cinnamon rolls with raisins."

"Cinnamon rolls? Haven't had any real good ones for a long time." Gunner frowned. Damn! Why did he say that. He still wanted to leave, but the baked goods sounded so good. "Maybe I can stay for a minute or two."

Effy smiled. Her blue eyes were not wary now. She was at home here and felt secure. Her eyes twinkled a bit at his shyness.

"Why don't you come back to my kitchen. The rolls are just out of the oven."

"Oh, no, I don't think I can do that."

"Why not, Gunner? We can sit at the table and talk."

He looked at her. He was entranced, all caught up with simply being near her and listening to her and watching her beautiful face. For a long moment he stared at her, then slowly he nodded.

"Good." Effy reached down and caught his hand. "Right back this way through the curtain. We were going to put a door on, but with a curtain I can hear if somebody comes in."

Gunner stiffened when she took his hand, but he didn't pull away. Effy moved toward the kitchen and he went with her, his arm frozen at his side.

"I hope you like my kitchen. I decorated it myself with wallpaper from Mr. Partridge's store."

The first room was a storage area, and the next open door led into a kind of kitchen that had been fashioned from another store room. A length of stove pipe extended through the wall for the small wood-burning cookstove. There was a table and chairs and a washstand and a small counter that had been patched together from scrap lumber.

"Not much, but it's all mine," Effy said.

"Your mother owns the building, and she lets me live here free. She also helps me pay the cost of running the library. Now a few other merchants are starting to contribute to the library fund as well."

She let go of his hand then, and he pulled it back as if to protect it. She went to the oven on the small stove and took out a pan of eight cinnamon rolls. They had been baked before and put back in the oven to stay warm.

She took two out and put them on small plates and placed them on the table. Effy sat in one of the chairs and pointed to the other one. Gunner looked around a moment as if he had been trapped, then sat and picked up the roll and took a bite of it. He chewed for a minute and grinned.

"Just like Ma used to make," he blurted, a fine smile cracking his face. He eagerly took another bite of the roll that had been smothered with brown-sugar frosting and walnuts and raisins.

"Your Ma still makes them like this," Effy said with a smile. "The fact is, she gave me the recipe because I liked them so much." Effy got up to pour cups of coffee from a pot that had stayed warm on the front of the cookstove.

Gunner sipped the coffee. Effy pushed

the sugar bowl at him and a spoon, and he took two portions of sweetener in his coffee. Neither of them spoke for a minute. Then Effy watched him until he looked up.

"Your mother hopes that you'll stay on here now that she's found you again," Effy said. "Will you be staying?"

"Dunno. Depends."

"Yes, I understand. You have friends you're traveling with. I know how important friends are."

"Do you have any friends?" Gunner asked.

Effy looked up, surprise showing on her face. "Well, your ma is about my best friend. Then there's a woman in the church choir that I like a lot. A few others."

"Any men friends?" Gunner asked.

This time she laughed and reached over and touched his hand. "Not right now, Gunner. But you're a man and I hope that you'll be my friend."

She watched him and Gunner looked away. He sighed, then looked back.

"Yes, I'd like to be your friend. All of my other friends are men."

"I understand that you ride the trail with them, Gunner. But I won't do that. I don't want to be that kind of a friend."

"You're an at-home friend," Gunner

said. "I know. Women stay at home, like my Ma."

By that time the cinnamon rolls were gone, but they continued to sip on the coffee. With no warning, Gunner stood.

"Time for me to go. I got to walk around the rest of the town."

Effy sat there watching him. "I understand. Will you come back and see me? Will you stop by this afternoon for another cup of coffee?"

Gunner felt confused. No woman had ever asked him to come see her. He was upset and afraid and desperately wanted out of that room. Quickly he nodded and bolted for the front door.

Effy sat there watching him go. She smiled softly as she heard the outside door close. She liked that big moose of a man. Effy hadn't the slightest idea why, but he was so alone and so afraid and so shy around women that she wanted to mother him. But she wanted more than just that. For a moment she wondered what he would look like with his clothes off.

Effy laughed as a relief for her own tense nerves, and cleaned the table and put the dishes in her dishpan on the counter. She would see as much of Gunner Johnson as she could. Who could tell what might happen?

★ ★ ★

Back at the hotel, Eagle wanted to work on his book, but found his room ill-equipped for writing. However, when he gave the hotel clerk two dollars, the man magically produced a writing desk for his room. Now the Comanche settled down to his first full day of writing his second book. He had talked with Laurita Benjamin at the Denver Library before he left, and they had decided that his second book should be on the sacred rituals of the Comanche people.

He stared at the long yellow pad of paper and took a deep breath. There was so much he wanted to write down, so much of the rich traditions and rituals of the Comanche People that he wanted to record before it was lost forever as the white man swept the Comanche farther and farther west onto the reservations.

He would write about simple things, like how when a Comanche hunter killed a deer or elk, he would take the head of the animal and turn it to the east. For it was from the east where the sun rose and brought with it life-giving light and warmth that made all things grow and helped another deer to grow to replace the one that had been sacrificed to supply food to the tribe.

Eagle would also write about how when a Comanche took his place at a formal meal he would cut off a small piece of the food and hold it skyward as a symbolic offering to the great spirit. Then to complete the ritual, he would bury the piece of blessed food in the ground so it could help nourish more food.

Eagle realized that just the ceremonies would not be enough. He had to explain what each ceremony was for, who performed it, how the priest and the medicine man often took part, and how the entire ceremony fit into and formed and motivated the Comanche way of life. It would involve much more than a simple cataloging of ceremonies.

He felt that Laurita back in Denver had understood this when they talked about the ceremonies book, and now he did as well. He put down his pencil and began to remember his days as a Comanche on the plains of Texas. That last summer before he was captured, he was only 12 and had nothing better to do than to practice with his bow and arrow and lance and to train his pony so that it would grow up to be a spirited, brave war pony.

He remembered one day when the tribe celebrated a great ceremony to purify the warriors before a raid. With that memory in mind, he took a pencil in hand and began to write his book about the Comanche ceremonies.

Willy Boy had spent most of his first day in Flagstaff at the Cork And Tap Saloon just across the street from the hotel. Willy Boy had taken a bath that morning, put on his best black suit, vest, white shirt, and tie, and bought a new white cowboy hat to top off the outfit.

He played two games of poker and lost five dollars, then caught the eye of the girl he had been watching. He knew she was a whore, but she was the youngest and smallest of the six in the saloon. She flounced over to him and bent down so he could see down the front of her dress, but her breasts were modest even though they were pushed up by the stays of her corset.

"Anything I can do for you, cowboy?" she asked. He told her to bring them two whiskeys, one for her and one for him and tossed her 50 cents. She brought two drinks back, didn't offer him any change, and smiled sweetly as she sat down across from him at a table for two.

"You're new in town," she said. "I'm Frieda."

Because the members of the Willy Boy Gang had all taken to using different names when they registered in hotels in towns, Willy Boy grinned and said, "Hi, Frieda. Call me Charley. You gonna be busy for the next three days?"

Frieda took a drink of her tea that was supposed to look like whiskey and smiled.

"You look like a swell, but do you have sixty dollars? That's my price, three days at twenty bucks each, and a bargain at three times the price."

Willy Boy slid a bill on top of the table and let her take a look at it. It was a $100 note.

"Land O'Goshen! Looks like you got the cash. Why don't we make it for five days?"

"Might not be around that long. We take it a day at a time. I might get tired of you. Or you might not be as good as you look."

"No worry there, cowboy, I'm terrific in and out of bed. Better than that even. What's first, upstairs?"

"No, Frieda, first I want to go on a picnic. A nice quiet picnic with a basket lunch, a one-horse shay, and a slow drive down along the river."

"We don't got much of a river, just a little creek, but, land sakes, it should do. You give me five dollars, and I'll go rent the rig and get the lunch and everything. Be back in half an hour."

Willy Boy gave her a ten-dollar eagle coin and she grinned, reached over and kissed his cheek. Then she hurried upstairs to change clothes and tell the woman she worked for about her great luck.

An hour later they drove the smart four-wheeled shay along the creek. Frieda directed him to a spot just off the river road and behind some brush where they couldn't be seen from the trail. The small stream chattered and bounced along over a bed of gravel and boulders directly in front of them.

Frieda spread a blanket near the water on the grass and lugged out the picnic basket. She opened a bottle of wine and then spread out sandwiches and a big dish of potato salad, a pot of beans, large dill pickles, and a dish of still hot fried chicken.

"We gonna eat first or what?" she asked.

Willy Boy stared at the food and patted her breasts, then grabbed a drumstick. "I always eat first, Frieda, remember that."

Juan had been sitting on the chair outside the Partridge General Store for an hour when he felt someone staring at him. His right hand eased down beside his six-gun as he glanced around casually. The man watching him was only a dozen feet away, and he had familiar dark skin and black moustache — a Mexican.

Juan looked up at the man and made a small nod. The other Mexican did the same and then moved his head slightly toward the alley. A moment later he vanished into the shadows of the valley.

Juan waited a moment, then stood and wandered down past the rest of the general store and turned in at the alley. He held his hand near his weapon as a precaution. Once past the splash of sunshine, he could see easily in the shadows. The Mexican leaned against the wall and chuckled.

"You take no chances, amigo," he said in Spanish.

"I am alive because I have been careful," Juan answered in the same language. "How come you are here so far north?"

"I live here. I work for my patron who is good to me, even though some of the townspeople spit on me. And you?"

"I come with my anglo friends. I won't be here for long."

"But still you must eat and rest your head. You're welcome to stay with me. *Mi casa es su casa.*"

Juan hesitated. "You know nothing of me or of my family."

"You are a countryman in a hostile land. That's enough. Come and meet my family."

Juan nodded. The other was about five years older than Juan's 21 years. He had an easy self-confidence that Juan liked.

"My name is Hernando Escobar. I work for Mrs. Johnson at the mill. I am the best saw filer in the country, so I work at night when the others are sleeping."

Juan lifted his brows. "Did you see or hear anything the night the man died at the mill?"

"Yes, but I'm only the Mexican, so no one asked me. It is not my affair."

They walked out of the alley to Arizona Street and turned south. They came to Ponderosa Street and on that corner sat a small white house with lots of flowers in the front yard. It had a white picket fence and was easily the best kept house on the short block. Beyond it and on the far corner of the same block, Juan saw a three-story house looming over all the rest.

"Mi Casa," Hernandez said opening the gate on the picket fence in front of the small house. "Come in and meet my family. You're welcome to take your meals here and stay. We can find a spare bed."

That evening after the meal of real Mex-

82

ican food, the two men sat on the porch and watched the sun set over the mountains.

"It is a good place to live," Hernando said. "There is plenty of rain and cool weather. We've even gotten used to the snow. And Maria can grow all kinds of flowers in the summer."

"True," Juan said. But the talk about the killing still bothered him. "I have a friend who is helping Mrs. Johnson deal with her company," Juan said. "He thinks someone killed the gringo at the mill. He says it was no accident."

"That is true," Hernando said.

"If you know about it, you must tell Mrs. Johnson or my friend," Juan said.

Hernando shrugged. "It is between the gringos. It is not my problem."

Juan sighed. "How long have you been in the *Estados Unidos*, Hernando?"

"Over a year now. It is good here."

"Part of it being good is that each of us helps look after the rest. It is not like in Mexico where the *federales* rule and everyone tries to protect himself from them. Here the people rule, the laws are just and fair. If we live here, we must live by the American laws and the way the gringos do things. It is your duty to tell Mrs. Johnson what you know."

Hernando frowned for a few seconds, then sighed. "It is so good here. The man I saw with the dead man could fire me, or even kill me." He looked at Juan. "But you are right. I have learned something of the gringo laws. They are not perfect, but they are far better than the *federales*." He looked at the clear night sky and the millions of stars that shined in the black sky. At almost 7,000 feet Juan thought he could reach up and touch a star.

Hernando nodded. "*Sí,* you are right, amigo, you are right. I will stop by on my way to work tonight and tell Mrs. Johnson what I saw."

Chapter Six

The Professor slipped out the back door of the general store and ran down the alley toward Arizona Street. There he turned north and trotted to the end of the block which led him to Sawmill Street.

In another five minutes, he was inside the mill office, and he was sure that no one had followed him. Who would be watching him? Who but a damn bounty hunter had any reason to suspect him of anything? All the members of the gang had suffered a lot at the hands of wild-eyed kids trying to earn $10,000 reward money.

The Professor asked Nancy the bookkeeper who the four largest customers were. He did it quietly and told her not to tell anyone about it. She wrote down the names and addresses. One was a lumberyard in Albuquerque, New Mexico Territory, another a building contractor in the same town. The third was another contractor right there in Flagstaff, and the last one was over at the edge of Texas in a town called Claymore.

The Professor asked Nancy if there were any spare hats in the office. She showed him one, a dirty beat-up old felt hat with almost no shape at all. One of the men had used it when it was raining she said. The Professor took it, slipped out of his dark suit jacket, then took off his matching vest and hung them over a chair.

"Pair of gents have been interested in where I went this morning. Figure I'll make it a little harder to find me."

Nancy frowned. "Does this have anything to do with poor Mr. Franklin's death?"

"Not sure. But I'd rather be alive to find out one way or the other. Don't tell anyone where I'm going."

"Oh, I won't. I don't know."

He left with a grin and walked rapidly away and down to Sawmill Street, where he turned right along the tracks to the small railroad station at the end of the tracks. It was only a hutch of a building, just big enough for one ticket seller, the telegraph operator, and a small safe for the Railway Express agent.

The Professor sent three telegrams to the three out-of-town customers requesting the same information: "Auditing the books of Johnson Lumber. Please send the undersigned at this station, the total of your payments to Johnson Lumber for each of the last two complete months. Strictest of confidence. N. Brown, Auditor."

The telegraph operator took the message and the three addresses and charged the Professor 40 cents a word for each of the wires. Then the Professor walked down Arizona Street to the firm he had noticed before, Wilson Building Contractors.

The building fronted on Arizona Street almost behind the Flagstaff Hotel. A pretty redheaded young woman came up to a high counter that stretched across the large room. Most of the rest of the inside of the building was taken up with walled-off offices.

"Yes, sir?" she asked.

"I'd like to see your president or manager, please."

"And what would that be about?"

"It concerns your account with Johnson Lumber."

A heavy-set man at a desk looked up and frowned. "Stella, I'll talk to the gent. Wally would just send him to me anyway." The man stood and waved the Professor through a swinging gate in the end of the counter.

"I'm Philpot, head bookkeeper here. Anything that has to do with the Johnson Lumber account is my prime business. Without them we couldn't build an outhouse."

He shook hands with the Professor, who introduced himself as Nate Brown. The company man waved him to a chair beside his desk.

The Professor quietly told him what information was needed. Philpot nodded. "No trouble at all. Take me about two minutes to put that together. We keep damn good records here, and the Johnson Lumber has several ledger sheets all its own. Just a shake."

He opened a ledger and made some notes, then quickly added up two columns of figures. He handed the Professor the paper.

"Here we are. Two months ago was slower for us, but we wrote drafts to Johnson Lumber for 12,487 dollars. Last month it was almost fourteen thousand."

The Professor memorized the figures, then pushed the paper into his pants pocket. He had taken his hat off when he came in and held it at his side.

"Thanks, Mr. Philpot. This is exactly what I need. I'm doing a small audit, and it always pays to have outside information."

"To double-check your people, I know how that can be. We had to let a man go about a year ago for some money trouble."

The Professor thanked him and walked out of the office. He checked Arizona Street both ways, but saw no one. The two men who had been following him evidently had lost the scent and maybe their enthusiasm.

He retraced his steps up to Sawmill Street and back to the mill office. There, upon the Professor's request, Nancy quickly totaled up the payments from Wilson Builders she had received for the past two full months.

She wrote down the figures and the Professor thanked her. Less than $4,000 had been recorded on the books as payment from Wilson two months earlier, and the previous month's total was listed as just over $5,000. The Professor pulled a poker face to hide any surprise and asked another question.

"How are your orders handled, and who does the billing and keeps the accounts receivable?"

Nancy pointed to Mace Duncan's office. "Mr. Duncan takes care of most of that, especially on the larger accounts. He handles all four of those I gave you the addresses on."

"Isn't that a little unusual, the manager doing billing and accounts receivable?"

"Oh, yes, but Mr. Duncan said he used to be an accountant, and he can do the work quicker and better than anyone here. The man he fired about a year ago had been doing most of that work, and he said it was unfair to burden anyone else with the extra duties."

The Professor nodded. The bastard had covered all of his bases. He sent out the correct invoices, entered a smaller figure on the company books and the accounts receivable, then paid that amount out of the checks when he took them out of the mail. He must have billed in sections so there would be a number of checks for each large customer. A neat little method to swindle the company. The cheating and thievery would be easy to prove. But what the Professor wanted most was to nail the bastard for killing Ross Franklin.

For that he was going to need some help.

The morning train from the east didn't arrive until nearly noon that day. Bert Filmore stepped down from the Atlantic and Pacific passenger car and stared at the makeshift town. He snorted, carried his carpetbag to what he figured was the town's one hotel, and registered. As he did, he scanned the list of other guests on the long page. There wasn't one of the Willy Boy Gang names there.

Deputy Sheriff Andrews had warned him about that. They seldom used their real names. It was too risky with all the wanted posters out on them. He went downstairs and checked the hotel dining room. It wasn't much and he thought he'd probably eat somewhere else. None of the men he searched for were in the dining room.

Bert left the hotel and walked north on Main Street. He found a café three doors up and went in. It was small and looked clean. He had some soup and a plate of toast and jam. None of the men he wanted were eating there. They had to eat somewhere. He hurried his small meal and surveyed the rest of the town.

Bert found three more places to eat, but couldn't spot any face or form that matched his descriptions. The men had to eat somewhere and sleep. Unless they had rented a house and set up housekeeping, but he doubted they had since it wouldn't be practical so they must eat early or late.

He checked out the largest and best eatery, the Flagstaff Restaurant, and went in and ordered a cup of coffee and a doughnut. He sipped at the brew and watched.

By three o'clock he hadn't seen anyone who could match the easiest three to identify. Eagle the Indian, Juan the Mexican, and Gunner the giant would be the most likely ones to spot.

As Bert walked the street, he saw no one he could even suspect. He asked someone where the sheriff's office was and got only a chuckle. He went into a store and asked the clerk. He found out there was no lawman in the small town.

"We don't even have a town marshal," the slender man in the J. A. Overbear Boots and Shoes store said. "Can't afford it yet. Maybe next year if we keep growing."

"No lawman at all? No jail. What about criminals?"

"Things get bad enough, the county sheriff comes in. I don't rightly know where he is now. Counties keep changing up here."

Bert knew then he would have to find the Willy Boy Gang on his own. He left the store and settled into a chair next to the café beside the saddle shop and watched the patrons. He sat there for two hours, then went inside the café and ordered a sparse dinner. He didn't want to spend any more of his cash money than he had to.

Bert thought of putting up some of the wanted posters he had in the bottom of his suitcase. But he decided against it because it was better not to let the gang know anybody was after them and this close. He shook his head. The Willy Boy Gang might not even be there anymore. They might have left on the stage and be half way to California.

Bert ordered the country beef stew, a cup of coffee, and two slabs of bread and called it quits. He hadn't seen any of the members of the Willy Boy Gang. If they were in town, he had no idea where they could be.

The rest of the evening he would try the saloons. At least two of the men were gamblers. They wouldn't be able to keep away from the gaming tables and the whores. Tonight he would find at least one of them, and he would capture him and use him as bait to get the others. He didn't want just one of them dead, he wanted all five of them!

The first saloon he tried had nickel beer, and he made one mug last for almost an hour. He watched the drinkers, but mostly surveyed the men playing poker and faro and some of the other games of chance. One man was well-dressed, with a black suit, a vest, and a bowler hat sitting on the table beside him. He had a gold watch chain and fob and the look of a real dandy.

The man was winning.

Bert watched him for ten minutes, then asked the barkeep who the fancy man was. The bartender was a rough-looking man with a scar over one eye and a smashed nose. He glared at Bert and shook his head.

"None of my business, mister. You want to know who he is, go over and ask him." The bartender stared at Bert so hard he slid back from the stand-up bar and drifted away. He asked two more men before he found one who knew the man.

"Oh, sure, I know him. That's Fancy Dan Jenkins. Best damn gambler in this town. He comes up from Phoenix once a month to trim the local suckers. He's good, but some say he cheats a little. Don't say it to his face, of course."

Bert began watching the others. One man was tall enough to be the Professor. But he wore a slouch hat that looked like it had been through a stampede. He wore a white shirt, but no vest and no coat or tie. Besides, this man was losing. The Professor was supposed to be good with cards.

He checked the rest of the men, sighed, and walked out of the saloon. There Bert leaned against the wall of the saloon. It was dark out now. Most of the businesses were shut down. Only the saloons and whorehouses were still open. Somehow he didn't think finding the gang would be this hard. They were in town, he knew it. He could feel them. But why couldn't he find even one out of the five?

He shook his head and moved down the street to the next gambling hall in the Logger's Rest Saloon.

Hernando Escobar didn't go to his saw filing job at the mill until eight o'clock in the evening. He left his small white house about seven-thirty that night. He kissed his wife Maria, picked up his two boys and hugged them, then went out the door.

He had struggled with his conscience and finally decided what he should do. It was his civic responsibility to report lawbreakers. That meant he had to talk to Mrs. Johnson. He was determined now. Even if the man found out about his testimony, it would be too late for him to hurt

Hernando or his family.

He nodded as he walked around the block to the big house where Mrs. Johnson lived. He was nearing the front gate when someone came out of the shadows. The moonlight glinted off metal in the man's hands.

"This is a six-gun, Mexican. Don't move or I'll shoot you full of holes. You understand?"

"Yes."

"Turn around and walk across the street and then head for the timber. You've been causing too much trouble around town."

Hernando had heard the flat dead voice of the *federales* too often. This man sounded the same; Hernando could tell he was a paid killer. He was doing a job for someone and he had no interest in anything but finishing the job and getting the money. To do what he said meant a sure, quick death, and Hernando wasn't ready for that.

He slowed and pointed back at the big white house. "Mrs. Johnson is on the porch watching us," he said. As soon as the gunman turned his head for a quick look at the house, Hernando sprinted away.

The gunman yelped at the fleeing man as he turned back. Without taking aim, he fired three times. Then he could not see his victim anymore. The gunman ran in the same direction Escobar had gone and stopped and listened, but heard nothing. He ran one way, then the other. There were no close buildings, only open space and the darkness.

The gunman made a circle and listened, then stopped and listened again. He was sure he had hit the man at least once. He swore and pushed his six-gun back in leather. He'd have to tell his boss that he hit the man, but he wasn't sure if the man was dead. He turned and walked away toward Main Street.

Hernando lay where he had hidden under a small flush of brush. He had held his breath twice when the killer's footsteps had come within three feet of his hiding place. Now he waited five minutes until he was sure the man was gone. Twice he passed out.

He struggled to get out of the brush. Two of the bullets the paid killer fired had hit him. One had struck his leg and broken the bone, he was sure because he couldn't walk. He would have to crawl to Mrs. Johnson's house. How far was it?

As he crawled, he imagined that harpies clustered around him and their black wings beat at his consciousness. He was so tired. He drifted in and out of reality. Each time he came fully aware, he crawled a few more yards toward the lights of the house. It was so far away! It must be at least a mile.

For a moment he wondered where the other bullet hit him. It wasn't in his chest or torso. Then the headache came and he breathed a prayer to the Holy Mother. The bullet wound was on his head. Somehow it hadn't killed him. But would it do the job before he could get to the house?

He pushed with his good leg and slid another foot across the dirt of the street toward Mrs. Johnson's place. It was so far away!

He heard the jangle of harness as a light rig came up Main Street. He wanted to cry to the people on it, but it turned down Ponderosa. No help there. He thought of calling out anyway, but there were no houses close to him. The schoolhouse was behind him, and the big lot around Mrs. Johnson's house was empty. No one would hear.

He pushed hard with his left foot, sliding his body through the dust of the street. His right leg hit something and he screeched in pain; then the darkness became inky black and he wasn't sure where he was. He tried to crawl again, but couldn't move. The darkness closed in quickly until at last he gave a sigh and let his cheek fall to the dirt of the Arizona street.

Chapter Seven

Earlier that same afternoon, Gunner took a small box of books down to the library. His mother had smiled when she asked him if he could do that for her. Mrs. Johnson knew that Gunner had no idea she was pushing him toward Effy. She had figured the two as a perfect match even before Gunner came back to town. Now it seemed to be working out moderately well.

The big push would be up to Effy since she was staring squarely into the realization that she could be an old maid at 24. But she knew that she wasn't the prettiest or the best-formed single girl in town, so she wasn't sure of her chances with Gunner.

Unaware of his mother's matchmaking and Effy's longing, Gunner took the box of books from his mother the two blocks to the little library. When he strode in, Effy was delighted to see him.

"Gunner," she said, "just the man I was

hoping would come. I need to make some more bookshelves and I just can't pound these nails in the wall. Some nice men from the sawmill brought me the boards yesterday, but I'm all thumbs when it comes to sawing and hammering."

"Can I help do it?" Gunner asked.

Effy smiled sweetly and said, "Gunner, that would be a tremendous boost for me. I have the wood all laid out over here on the floor. It'll be our second wall of books. Next we'll have to make islands for the books. That'll be harder, but maybe you can help me figure it out, too."

She showed Gunner where she wanted the shelves and how far apart they should be. Gunner stared at the boards a minute, then looked at the other shelves and began to saw and pound away. Although he had it all laid down on the floor, Effy wasn't sure what he was doing, but it looked as if it might work. However it came out, she knew that she was going to praise him to the heavens.

A woman who was writing a special letter and wanted to be sure of her spelling came in looking for a dictionary, and Effy checked one out to her for a week. After that, Effy sat and watched Gunner. He seemed like a puppy or a big overgrown boy. But she had seen the look in his eyes when she kissed his cheek once. She intended to fan that smoldering desire into a flame one of these days when the time was right. With Gunner that would be the most important element.

"Gunner, that's coming along just fine. Don't you think it's time we stop and have some coffee? I made a new batch of cinnamon rolls this morning. I put a white frosting on them and raisins, too."

Gunner looked at her. "Right now before I'm done?"

"Right now. There's no big hurry on the shelves." He stood and she caught his hand and led him into the kitchen. She had done that twice now and he seemed to like her touch. He had never touched her, but he would.

She heated up the rolls until the top frosting began to melt and run down into the bread. Then she pulled the rolls from the oven and put two in front of Gunner on a plate with a fork. The coffee was always hot in her kitchen. She poured two cups and watched him.

"Good," Gunner said as he munched on the roll. "Just as good as Ma makes."

"Why thank you, Gunner, I appreciate that." She sipped her coffee. "I guess that you'll be staying on in town now. Your Ma sure can use your help with the mill and the lumbering business. She isn't a real good businesswoman, and she's the first to admit it."

"Stay on? Here?"

Effy smiled her best and nodded. "Yes, I just figured now that you found your ma again, and she had such a good business going here, that you'd want to stay and help her. Actually, the mill and the whole firm will be yours someday."

Gunner sat there thinking about what she had said.

"I hadn't thought about staying. The rest of the guys won't want to settle down here. The Professor said this was a jerkwater town. I'm not sure what that means, but I don't think he likes it here."

"He's more of a big-city man, probably," Effy said. She nibbled on part of a roll and sipped the coffee. "Gunner, you should think about staying here. Your mother really needs you. She spent a lot of time helping you grow up. Maybe it's time now that you repay some of that love and care by helping her."

Gunner frowned. "Yeah, maybe so. Hadn't thought about it much before."

"I really think you should. Your mother

isn't a young woman any more, Gunner." She got up and brought the coffee pot to refill his cup. As she reached across to his cup, her face came close to his. She put her hand on his shoulder to steady herself, and he turned to look at her.

"Oh my, I almost lost the coffee pot," she said. Their faces were only an inch apart. She pushed in and kissed his cheek, then leaned back and filled his cup.

When she came back from the stove, he was touching his cheek. "Why did you do that?" Gunner asked.

"What?" Effy said, pretending not to understand him.

"You know, kiss my cheek?"

"Why? I just wanted to. I like you, Gunner. I like it when you stop in and help me around the library. I like it when you tell me how good the cinnamon rolls are. I guess that means that I really like you, Gunner."

"Oh, well, I like helping you here."

"Have you ever had a girlfriend, Gunner?"

"A girlfriend?" Gunner said, confused.

"Some woman you liked and who liked you. Someone you spent some time with."

"Just one, but she was, well, I guess she was different from you."

"How do you mean, Gunner?"

"Well, my friend took me to her. She was in this little room over the saloon and the first thing she did was take her clothes off."

Effy giggled and pretended to hide her face. "No, Gunner, I didn't mean a woman like that."

"But I paid her and everything, and my friend said it was all right."

"It was all right, Gunner. I meant have you ever had a girl friend who you didn't pay?"

Gunner took the last bite of his second roll and slowly shook his head. "No, I guess not. I saw that other girl just three times."

"Gunner, I'd like to be your friend. Can I be your friend? All you have to do is come see me once in a while and help with the books and the shelves. And, of course, eat my cinnamon rolls. Maybe you could come to supper sometimes. I'm a good cook."

Gunner fidgeted on the chair. He looked at her from the corner of his eyes. "I won't have to pay you?"

"No, not a cent."

"And I guess that means you won't take your clothes off."

Effy giggled again. She hadn't giggled in years and it felt good. "No, Gunner, I won't embarrass you by taking off my clothes. So can we be friends?"

Gunner nodded, then he smiled. "Yes, friends."

"Good. There is one other thing that friends do, men and women friends. Sometimes they kiss each other. Would you like to kiss my cheek, Gunner?"

"It wouldn't hurt you?"

"Not a bit. In fact, I'd really like you to kiss my cheek."

She got up and came over beside him and leaned down. Gunner lifted his brows, looked around to make sure nobody saw him, then he leaned in and pecked a kiss on Effy's cheek.

"Good, thank you, Gunner. Now I feel more like your special friend. Let me put the dishes away, and I'll help you with those bookshelves."

It was nearly supper time when they got the last shelf nailed into the frame and lifted the set of shelves against the wall. Gunner nailed one cleat through the middle shelf and into the wall so that shelves wouldn't fall down.

"Great, we did it!" Effy shouted as he finished driving the nail. She ran to him, threw her arms around him, and kissed his cheek. Gunner was stunned by her action. Effy let go of him and stepped back.

"That's just wonderful, Gunner. Now we have room for three hundred more books."

She looked at the wind-up clock on the small desk. "Oh, goodness, look at the time. Would you like to stay to supper with me?"

Gunner took a step back from her and shook his head. "No, I have to get home. My mother is waiting for me." He turned and fled out the door.

Effy watched him go with a knowing smile. She had to remember just how shy he was, despite his asking her if she was going to take off her clothes if they were friends. She had to move slowly if she wanted to get Gunner Johnson where both she and his mother wished him to be.

The horseman riding up Main Street almost turned on Ponderosa, but he decided to ride on down Main and past Mrs. Johnson's place just to marvel at it. He was 50 feet from it when he saw a dark shape at the edge of the street.

Curious, he angled his mount that way and saw it was a man. The rider came up to the man and watched him a minute. He wasn't moving. He wondered if it was some kind of a trap. He drew his six-gun and eased off his mount and pushed the man's leg with his foot.

Nothing happened. He could see one hand, but the other was crumpled under the form. Keeping the Colt aimed at the figure, the rider knelt and touched the man's cool face. He pushed his fingers where the artery in the neck should be pumping blood. He could feel nothing.

Then he saw the wound on the side of the man's head next to the ground and the pool of dark red blood that had formed there. He jumped back, startled. Then he leaped up, caught the reins of his horse, and ran for the big house. He banged on the door until he heard someone coming.

A woman opened the door, and he knew she was Mrs. Johnson because he had seen her before.

"A man's been shot in the head. He's down in the street over there and I think he might be dead. Come watch over him so no rig hits him in the dark. I'm going to ride for the doctor."

The man whirled, not waiting for a response, and raced back down the sidewalk and through the gate. He scrambled on his horse and rode for the downtown area.

No stranger to tragedy and death, Harriet Johnson didn't hesitate to go to where the man lay. She pulled a scarf from the hall, wrapped it around her head and shoulders, and hurried out the door to the street. She found the man and knelt beside him. Gently she felt for a pulse, but couldn't find one at his throat or temple. She tried his wrist, but found no pulse there either. She pinched the man's nose closed, but there was no struggle for breath. The man was dead.

She waited in the street until the doctor rode up. He confirmed her suspicions in a moment. He moved the lantern he had brought so they could see the man's face.

"Oh, no!" Harriet Johnson wailed.

"Hernando Escobar," Doc Marston said. "He works for you, don't he, Mrs. Johnson?"

She nodded. "Yes, he's my saw filer. One of the best workers I've ever had. Who would want to harm him? He is a — he was a wonderful man, a good husband and father."

She stood. "Well, I better go see his wife before she hears from someone else. The poor dear. I don't know what she'll do now with her two small boys."

Doc Marston got up from the ground. The man who first found the body had returned as well. Marston looked at him. "Stay here until I send the undertaker for him," the doctor said. He picked up the reins of the horse and decided to walk back to his office. It was only about a block. "Be easier walking than getting up on that damned animal again," he said.

Mrs. Johnson walked back to her house and opened the safe Karl had installed in the pantry behind a rack of tinned goods. She took out five $20 bills and closed the safe. Then she walked with deliberate steps toward the small white house on the far side of the block.

What a tragedy! Hernando was such a fine young man. He was such a good worker. Some people in town shunned him because he was Mexican, but she had nothing but good things to say about him. His wife would be devastated.

Harriet Johnson had always thought of herself as a strong woman, but she shivered and hesitated before she knocked on the white door. A moment later, Maria came to the door, her pretty face curious.

"Yes? Oh! Mrs. Johnson. Come in." She was flustered and suddenly nervous, wondering why Mrs. Johnson had come to her home.

Inside Mrs. Johnson sat down on a chair

and urged Maria to sit down. She could think of no delicate way to say it. "Maria, there's been a tragedy and Hernando has been killed."

Maria's eyes went wide. She shook her head. "It can't be. He left here not an hour ago. He said he had to stop by and see you before he went to work. He said —" Mrs. Johnson caught her hands and held them. Slowly Maria's face dissolved into sorrow and anguish and tears, and she fell against the larger woman. She sobbed for three or four minutes, then pushed back.

"You must tell me it is not true!"

"I'm sorry, Maria. He might have been coming to see me. Someone shot him near my house. I don't know who or why, but I guarantee that we will find out."

Maria collapsed and Harriet caught her, then helped the sobbing woman through a door to one of two bedrooms. She had just put Maria on the bed when someone knocked on the front door.

Mrs. Johnson walked to the door and opened it. A Mexican man she did not know stood there. He showed surprise at seeing a white woman.

"Oh. Is Maria here? I had supper with the family, but I forgot my hat when I left. It must be right here."

Mrs. Johnson's mind was spinning. Another Mexican man. Gunner had spoken of a Mexican man in his group, what was his name? Juan?

"Are you my son Gunner's friend Juan?" she asked.

Juan looked up quickly in surprise. "Yes, I know Gunner Johnson."

"What do you know of Maria and Hernando?"

"I met them yesterday. Hernando invited me to supper. They are good people. He works for you as a saw filer."

"He did. But tonight while he was coming to see me, he was shot dead in the street."

"No!"

"I'm afraid so. Did he say anything about why he wanted to see me tonight?"

Juan felt a growing anger in his belly. He looked away to let some of the hatred drain from his face. When he turned back he was in control again.

"I think so. He said he knew that Ross Franklin did not die in a fall. He saw the man who killed him. He didn't tell me who it was, just said the man who did it could make trouble for him. He said he would come and see you tonight before he went to work."

"He didn't quite make it. I was playing the piano and I thought I heard a shot. I stopped playing, but I heard nothing else so I went on with my practicing. Then someone came to the door about a half hour later. Hernando was shot in the head. He must have died quickly."

Juan motioned to the other room. "Maria. You've told her?"

"Yes. She's shaken, angry. Don't worry about them. I'll take care of them. I have that big house with no one in it. I'll have them move in with me as soon as Maria wants to."

They stared at each other a few moments.

"I just wish Hernando had told me who he saw. He said he saw someone carrying the body to the cut-off saw. That's all he would say."

"Now two good men have died. Your friend, Mr. Brown, is helping me. But so far we can't prove much. He told me he has some evidence, but wants to make sure who killed Ross." She shook her head and turned away. "I can't believe that something like this is happening in Flagstaff. We've never had trouble like this."

Juan tightened his jaw and his eyes turned cold and hard. "Mrs. Johnson, if

there's anything I can do for Maria or her boys, you let me know. Right now I think I better find the — Nate Brown and tell him what happened. I'm sure he'll be concerned."

Chapter Eight

After searching half the town, Juan at last located the Professor in a small saloon called the Four Aces, which stood all the way down by Sawmill Street. The Professor wore his old hat and a blue-jean jacket. Juan signaled to him, and the Professor sat out a hand and went to the bar. Quickly Juan told him of his talk with Hernando and of the man's death.

The Professor nodded. "Somebody is damn smart or whorehouse lucky. They could have wondered if Hernando knew anything about Franklin's death since he worked nights at the mill. There was a chance he saw something. The killers could have had him tailed. If he did anything unusual, like go to the boss's house, he'd be taken out."

"Anything I can do to help?" Juan asked. "This thing is personal now. I liked Hernando and his family."

"This is getting to be more than penny ante," the Professor said. "I have a strong feeling that the bastards don't just want to steal a lot of money anymore. I bet they want the whole mill now."

Juan nodded. "Let's go check with Mrs. Johnson. There might be something we can do tonight."

They left the saloon by the rear door, worked between buildings to First Street, and walked quickly south toward Ponderosa Street and the Johnson mansion.

Staying in deep shadows, Juan and the Professor went up to the back door and knocked. Juan had to knock several times before someone came to the door.

"Who is it?" a voice asked, followed by the unmistakable click of a six-gun cocked on full.

"Mrs. Johnson, it's Juan and Nate Brown." They heard the bolt slide open and the door swung out. The two dark figures slipped inside in a moment, and Mrs. Johnson closed the door behind them and threw the bolt.

Mrs. Johnson nodded at the two. "Gunner's in the parlor. The shades are down. Let's go in there and talk."

Gunner grinned and waved as his two friends came into the room.

"Hey, it's like a celebration. Two of my good friends are here."

"Yes, Gunner, but it's not a celebration. One of your mother's workers was killed tonight. We need to talk about it."

"Oh, all right." Gunner sat down and listened.

The Professor told Mrs. Johnson his theory that the killer must have watched Hernando and killed him when he changed his normal behavior pattern by coming to see his employer.

"Could have been the same man who killed Franklin," Juan said. "Or the first killer could have hired somebody to do this one. This one might have been done by a professional since a gun was used."

Mrs. Johnson stared at them. "Would you like some coffee? Sometimes I think better when I can sip on some." They all went into the kitchen, where Gunner started a small fire in the wood-burning range, and they waited for the coffee to boil.

"Mrs. Johnson, has anyone tried to buy your business lately? Anyone made you an offer?"

"Several people did the month after Karl died. But there haven't been any since then." She frowned. "Oh, there was one, but he wasn't serious."

"Who?" Juan asked.

"One day we were at the office talking

117

about the business, and Mace said he'd sure like to have a business like this someday. He said he'd give me fifty thousand for it. I told him it was worth three, maybe four times that much. He laughed as if he didn't believe me. As a joke, I told him I'd leave him the mill in my will."

The Professor turned around suddenly. "Your will?"

"It was just talk, banter. You know how things can get. It wasn't serious at all."

"Mrs. Johnson, do you have a will?"

"Well, now that you mention it, no. I didn't know where Gunner was, and I have no other living relations. Years ago I lost track of one section of the family. I think they were killed by Indians, but I can't find any record of their deaths."

"But since you have no will, somebody could fake a will and claim you had written it," the Professor said.

"Who would want to kill Ross Franklin and Hernando?" Juan asked.

"You have a lawyer, Mrs. Johnson?" the Professor asked.

"Yes, but I work with him mostly for the business."

"Tomorrow morning I suggest that you go see him early and have him draw up a will for you. Be sure it's sworn, witnessed, signed, sealed, and stored in one of those new safe boxes at the bank. The new ones take two keys to open; you keep one and the bank keeps one."

Mrs. Johnson poured the coffee and sat down at the table.

"Yes, Mr. Brown, I think that's sound advice. I'll go down first thing tomorrow. Land sakes, I don't really believe this. All this violence and murder right here in quiet little Flagstaff."

"Believe it," Juan said. The men sipped their coffee, then said good night and eased out the back door into the blackness.

"Mace Duncan?" Juan asked as they walked back toward the hotel.

"Sure as hell looks like it, but proving it is going to be a different bucket of worms."

They entered the Flagstaff Hotel separately, Juan first by the front, then the Professor through the side door. Nobody seemed to be watching the Professor as he went up the steps to the second floor and down the hall to his room. He walked the wooden-floored hallway quietly as he always did and paused outside his room. He was about to put his key in the lock when he heard a muffled cough from inside his room.

He had been standing half on the wall

side of his door, and now he shifted so his whole body was beyond the door. He hit the door knob with his hand rattling it, then jerked his hand back.

Almost before a new heartbeat, a shotgun blast ripped through the door, deadly double-ought buck shattering the thin panel, then a second round tore out what was left of the door.

The Professor pushed his hand around the jagged remains of the door and fired twice into the room; then he heard the window creak. He jolted around the splintered door and into his room.

He saw a man's legs leaving the window and fired a quick shot, but missed his target. The Professor raced to the window, which opened on a small ledge. Ten feet below the ledge was the ground at the side of the hotel in back of the butcher shop.

The Professor went through the window. As he stood on the ledge, someone fired a revolver at him, but the lead missed him. When he picked up the direction of the ambusher, he dropped off it, crumpled to his knees and rose, six-gun death still in his hand, then raced through the back lot behind the hotel toward Arizona Street.

Two shots came from ahead of him, and this time lead whizzed past him. He didn't return fire, only ran faster. His long legs ate up the ground, and he was within 20 feet of the bushwhacker before they reached Sawmill Street.

The Professor sighted low and fired twice. The second round plowed into his attacker's left leg and dumped him to the ground, where he rolled twice, then grabbed his leg, screaming in pain.

The Professor moved up slowly. "Drop the gun," he demanded.

"It's gone. You shot me!"

"Damn right, the only reason you aren't dead is because I want to talk with you. You tell me who hired you to shotgun me, and you have a chance of living."

"Sure. I tell you and then he kills me."

"That's a choice a bushwhacker for hire decides on when he takes money to do murder. Now who was he?"

"I've only been in town two days. I don't know his name."

The Professor had walked up cautiously and now he could see both the man's hands in the soft moonlight. He didn't have the six-gun. The Professor shot him in the right thigh and the man screamed again.

There was no one on the street. They were just past the Wilson Butcher offices and lot and 50 feet from Sawmill Street and the livery stables.

This time the Professor's voice was cold, low pitched and deadly. "Tell me who hired you or you get to die right where you lie."

"All right. Then you'll get me to a doctor, right? He was a big guy, the people in the bar knew him. I asked. They said his name —"

Two rifle shots broke into the silence of the moonlit night. The Professor jumped back. One of the rounds hit the dirt between his feet, and the other one ripped into the man on the ground.

The Professor knew the shots came from the side toward the livery, but he couldn't see any smoke, it was too dark. He had dropped to the ground and now he could hear movement, but it was too faint to give him a target. He lay where he was at the side of the street for five minutes and nothing happened. The killer was gone.

Quietly, he moved up to the bushwhacker. The rifle bullet had torn into the man's rib cage and splattered his heart over the inside of his chest. He would never bushwhack anyone else.

The Professor turned and trotted back to the hotel, through the vacant lot just down from it, and in the side door. The room clerk saw him coming and handed him a key.

"Seems someone used your room while you were out. This new one is just across the hall."

The Professor took the key without a word and ran up the steps. He found the other three members of the gang in his ruined room. They had lit a lamp and had packed up his belongings. Willy Boy grinned.

"Hey, looks like you're cutting right close to the bone on this murder job you were telling me about. Somebody is getting damned nervous."

Eagle nodded. "Any idea who the varmint might be?"

"An idea, but no proof. I'm moving across the hall. It's time we talked and tried to work out some ways to root out this killer."

Juan picked up the Professor's carpetbag. "I got all night. I want the man who put down Hernando."

They talked well into the night. From a half-dozen ideas, they at last settled on three steps to take. The first was that the Professor would confront Mace the next morning and tell him he had a month to get the Johnson Sawmill and Lumber Company income level up to where it should be or he would be fired. They hoped that would stir him up and make him do something wrong.

Chapter Nine

Bert Filmore sat in the hotel dining room staring at his empty plate. It had been a good breakfast, but his funds were shrinking and he hadn't found a single one of the five Willy Boy Gang members. They had to be in Flagstaff. He was sure of it.

Flagstaff was perfect for them. No law, no reason for any. It was the perfect hideout. They had all the money they needed so they didn't have to rob banks any more. He picked up his coffee cup and looked over it as a man with dark hair came into the dining room and stopped at the small counter where customers paid their checks.

The man was maybe five-nine, and he had dark black hair and strange dark skin. Not Negro dark, or Mexican, somehow he was different. Then the man turned as he talked to one of the waiters.

An Indian! He could be Eagle, the Comanche. All at once Bert was too nervous to stand up. He knew he should rush up with his six-gun out and take the man into custody. But where would he put him? There wasn't even a jail in this little town. He could simply shoot him down and wire home with the news that he had killed Eagle, one of the damned Willy Boy Gang. The whole town would hold a celebration. Twelve men had been killed in that town by the gang.

But Bert couldn't move. He tried once and dropped back in his chair. It looked like the Indian was ordering a meal. That was why Bert hadn't found him in the dining room. He slipped in, ordered and carried a tray back to his room. Damn him!

Bert had to follow him and find out which room he was in. He commanded himself to lift off the chair. He had already paid the waiter, so he walked out of the dining room trying not to look at Eagle.

He gave a sigh when he was past the Indian. He continued on to the chairs opposite the stairway. The Indian would have to walk by him to get to the rooms on the first floor. If he were on the second floor, he would take the stairs. Eagle wouldn't be watching behind himself as he carried his breakfast tray back to his room, so Bert would have no trouble following him. Bert wondered what the Indian did all by himself in the room all day. Maybe he had a woman with him. Yes, that would explain it.

About five minutes later, Eagle left the dining room with a tray holding two covered dishes and a glass of milk. He came directly toward Bert, then turned up the stairs. When he was near the top, Bert rose and followed him. He got just to the top of the steps when he saw Eagle open the door directly opposite his own room.

Bert couldn't believe it. He had been within spitting distance of the man and didn't even know it. Now all he had to do was decide what to do with him. It took a sheriff's wire to confirm a dead-or-alive corpse of a wanted man. Bert had no idea where the closest sheriff was. Would it be possible to take Eagle back to Texas alive?

"Oh damn!" Bert said softly. Nobody had told him it was going to be this complicated to capture the killers.

The rest of the day he watched Eagle's room out a crack of his open door. He discovered that Eagle stayed in his room all day except to go out for food. Once in the afternoon he went to the general store two doors down and bought two pads of paper and a fist full of pencils. Bert wondered what in hell the Indian was doing in his room all day.

The Professor made an early morning call on Mace Duncan at the mill office. Duncan didn't seem surprised to see the Professor, which could mean that he had used the rifle the night before himself. It could also mean that he had nothing to do with the attack, but the Professor doubted that.

"So, Mr. Brown, what can I do for you this morning?" Mace asked.

"First I'd like a cup of coffee, then we need to talk. I have two rather interesting items we need to go over."

Mace went to the door and asked Nancy to bring them coffee from the pot that was always hot on the back of a small wood-burning stove in the storage room. Then he came back and peaked his fingers in front of his face after he sat in the swivel rocking chair behind his desk. "So, you said you had two items?"

"Yes, somebody from Wilson Builders came over while you were gone. It seems they're having some trouble with one of their bookkeepers and there was some kind of irregularity with one of the drafts they wrote to us for lumber. We checked it with Nancy, but the amount of the check, some eight hundred dollars, doesn't show up anywhere on the general ledgers or our income ledger, or on their special page in the income ledger, or in the accounts receivables.

"What Mrs. Johnson and I are wondering is did this bookkeeper write a check to us and then simply cash it himself and keep the funds? It didn't seem even to be sent to us. At least it doesn't show up in any of the ledgers where it would if it had come through regular channels."

Mace scowled, but the Professor could tell he was trying to cover up something. "The eight-hundred-dollar check was an actual billing that Wilson Builders had paid and was cashed at the bank by Johnson Lumber," the Professor said.

Mace shook his head. "Damn, I don't know why that thief had to involve us. Obviously he must be stealing money from Wilson Builders. He just figured out a different way to do it. Did they say how they got on to him?"

"Something about the signature being faulty. Anyway, I told Mrs. Johnson that I would double-check with you, so it's in your hands."

The Professor watched Mace. He shook his head and walked to the window and back. "I just can't understand why somebody embezzling money would pick our firm to use as the blind. Oh, well, yes, I guess it does make sense. They write a lot of good-sized checks to us. One more might not have been noticed. Yes, it could be. I'll review their account today." He looked up. "Anything else?"

"Yes, I've about decided to join Aunt Harriet in the firm. I would bring in some new capital but you don't need to worry about that. What I am demanding, however, is that the income level come up to where it should be for a firm like this. My estimate is that the income level is at least one hundred percent too low. A sawmill this size should be producing enough lumber to sell at the going rate, which would mean double the income on the books.

"I told Aunt Harriet if the income takes a jump I'll be glad to come in. Otherwise, it looks like in a month or two this mill will be losing money, not making money. So, if you, as manager, can show a turnaround in thirty days, I'll be in with both feet."

The Professor stood, loving the part he was playing. "Now I know you can't do this at once, but there should be ways to adjust outflow and increase income. Give it a try." And with that, the Professor turned and walked out of the office without a good-bye or a backward glance.

Mace watched the broad shoulders of the man vanish out his doorway, and the manager's automatic smile drooped like a wilted flower. Turnaround! There was no reason for a turnaround. The mill was making more money than ever — most of it was going into his pocket. He peaked his fingers again and stared through them. Perhaps he was going to have to change his long-range plans.

Now that the woman's damned son had surfaced, it was going to be harder than ever. The widow having a fatal accident was one thing, but getting rid of two of them might raise a lot of suspicion. Especially when six months later a will turned up with him as the primary beneficiary. Oh, he'd put in a $1000 grant to the Flagstaff Library and another $1000 to the little mouse who ran it. But even so, somebody might get suspicious.

Damn it, they had eliminated one witness last night, but the main fly in the molasses now was this Nate Brown, and he seemed like a hard man to kill. So what did he do next? He walked to the window and watched a pair of logs splash into the pond. They were old growth ponderosa pine, four feet in diameter. Prime logs for sawmilling.

There was no way around it: Nate Brown had to die. Just how was the hard part. A fall off a horse? A buggy accident? What about a fire in the hotel or a wild shot by a drunk? Mace discarded each in turn. It had to be something common, ordinary, and it had to happen soon.

While Duncan was plotting how to kill, he returned to his work. He went through the mail and seemed to find fewer checks than usual coming through from the four best customers. They seemed to come in surges. He finished his day's work and stopped by at the bank just before it closed.

Warner Payne smiled as Mace came up to the teller's cage.

"Good afternoon, Mr. Duncan."

"Good afternoon, Mr. Payne. I need some change and these two drafts cashed."

The clerk took the list of change, dimes, quarters and one dollar bills, and counted out the $40 to match the two double eagles presented. Then he looked at the two bank drafts. Both were made out to the Johnson Lumber Company. Both had been signed by Duncan who signed all of the checks for deposit.

One was in the amount of $247 and the other for $544. Payne quickly added the two, reduced the $791 total by ten percent, and showed the figures to the sawmill manager. The clerk counted out the bills, fifties and twenties, to the total of $711 and showed Duncan the four $20 bills that he folded and slipped into his pocket.

"Yes, Mr. Payne; that seems to be correct. Thank you for your help."

"Thank you, Mr. Duncan. Always a pleasure doing business with you." They nodded and Mace Duncan walked out the front door with the money safely tucked away in his wallet. He carried the bag with the coins and change to take back to the mill office. He needed the change to accommodate the small builders who often came directly to the mill for their lumber.

He felt the bulge in his wallet and grinned. He had intended to settle down in Flagstaff, but now with the appearance of the son and Mr. Brown, he was forced to consider strongly other options.

He stopped by at the Flag Restaurant for an early supper. Twice he patted his favorite waitress on the bottom and she giggled. She came closer to bring his food.

"Tonight?" she asked. He looked down the front of her blouse as she bent over his table, but had to shake his head.

"Not tonight, sweetheart. I've got some problems to take care of. Maybe tomorrow."

She pouted prettily as she walked away swinging her bottom at him to show him what he was missing. Mace grinned watching her, then dove into his meal. That night he intended to count up precisely how much money he had and try to figure out exactly what he should do. If Brown died tomorrow night, then he might be able to reconsider. If not, he would have to leave quickly and quietly late some evening. He would go toward California. It would be too easy to wire down the rail line and have a sheriff on his neck if he went east.

He wasn't thinking about much that evening as darkness settled in and he walked up to his small house a half block from the mill. It was a rental, but at $15 a month, he couldn't complain.

Polly met him at the door wearing only a skirt, but he wasn't in the mood. "Get your clothes on and move out of here now. I can't afford you any more. Go back to the saloon. Right now. No arguments."

134

She pouted and coaxed, dropped her skirt and pleaded with him, but he pushed her away. He had too many troubles to worry about her. It took him an hour to get her out of his house. Then he kicked off his shoes and tipped a pint bottle of fine Tennessee sipping whiskey and relaxed. He would count his money after a short break.

A knock sounded on the front door. Mace sighed and went to answer it. But there was no one there when he opened it. He looked around, went out on the small porch and called softly. It was almost fully dark now and he saw no one. Perhaps some kids were playing a trick on him. It had happened once before.

In the next ten minutes the knocking on the front door came twice more. Twice he found no one there. Then while he was still at the front door, he heard someone at the back. He sprinted out of the front and around the side, but by the time he got to the rear of his small house, the back stoop was empty as well.

"Damned brats!" he yelled into the night. Then went inside and made sure his six-gun was fully loaded. He thought of putting salt into some shotgun shells but decided against it. He didn't want to kill some kid playing a prank by shooting him with a shotgun load of salt that refused to break up. That could ruin all of his plans.

He settled down in his chair after bolting both the front and back doors. Usually he didn't do that. He bet there weren't a half-dozen homes locked in Flagstaff any night of the week.

Suddenly, a whistle shrilled. It was the kind some police carried in big cities. The sharp whistle came again and then a third time.

The sound brought him out of his chair grabbing for the revolver. He cocked the hammer and looked around. He ran to the window. Before he could move the curtain aside some wild, hysterical laugh came from the other side of the house

What in hell was going on? Mace asked himself. Nothing like this had ever happened before. As he got to the middle of the living room he heard something hit the roof. It sounded as if someone had jumped on it. He rushed outside in front and snapped off a shot at the chimney. The bullet hit and whined away. When the sound of the shot died down, he could hear nothing. The night was deathly quiet.

He walked around the house, saw nothing out of the ordinary and went back in the front door and slid the bolt.

Nothing happened until he turned the light out about nine-thirty and dropped on the bed. Then the police whistle shrilled again, and he jolted upright in bed. Mace grabbed the six-gun from under his pillow.

The front door rattled as if someone were trying to get inside. He cocked the six gun and raced for the front door. Without thinking he fired through the door. It was a cheap one, and the .45 caliber bullet ripped through it with ease. Before he knew what he was doing, he fired again, then unbolted the door and looked out.

On the small front porch he found an envelope. His hands shook as he picked it up. He looked around at the darkness, but could see no one. Two lights still glowed in houses down the street, but that was all.

Back inside the house, with the front door bolted again, he tore open the envelope and looked at the piece of paper. It had writing on it. With fumbling fingers, he struck a match and held the paper so he could see it. There were four words on the paper, two names.

"Ross Franklin." Below that was written: "Hernando Escobar." The paper was bordered in black. He dropped it as if it was haunted.

Just then the kitchen window rattled and

Mace ran into the room and fired a round through the window. The breaking glass and the roar of his own weapon stopped him this time. He lowered the gun and held his head. He realized there was only one round left in his weapon.

Slowly he went back to his bedroom and lay on top of the covers. He reloaded the weapon and vowed he'd shoot the first person he saw around his house. He lay there panting, his head bursting with a mighty headache and his hands moving.

Four more times, just an hour apart, the doors and windows rattled and the police whistle shrilled in the night. Twice Mace had just fallen asleep when he was jolted awake again. About four o'clock he gave up, dressed, made a fire, and cooked breakfast. There were no more attacks on his house that night.

Chapter Ten

The next morning, Effy looked over the part of the bookcase Gunner had painted and put on her Sunday best smile.

"Gunner Johnson, that is just the best work of painting that this library has ever seen. I had to do the first shelves, and they were splotched and spotty. Thank goodness I could cover them up with the new books I got. This one is going to be just beautiful."

"About done. You sure that cherry pie wasn't for something special?"

"Well, you're right, Gunner. I'm saving it for the nicest, most generous, kindest man I know — Gunner Johnson. As soon as you get done there we'll stop and have some pie and coffee. It's almost ten o'clock in the morning anyway. I was surprised when you got here so early this morning."

Gunner looked worried for a moment. "You said we needed an early start."

"Gunner, I'm just teasing you. I always

tease the people I like the most. I was up and dressed and all ready for you, wasn't I?"

Gunner nodded. He finished the front edge of the last shelf and stepped back. He added some of the brown paint to two spots that he hadn't covered well and then put the top on the can.

"All done. Should be dry in four hours. Maybe sooner, but don't put any good books on it."

"Great, it's pie time."

As was her habit she caught his hand and led him through the store room into the kitchen, and this time on into another room that she had fixed up as a living room. It had a couch with a small low table in front of it, two chairs, and several pictures on the walls.

She aimed him at the couch. "Gunner, you sit here and I'll be right back with the pie and coffee. We can have it here and it won't cost us each twenty cents each like it did over at the café." She stopped and watched him, her face a bright smile. "Besides, Gunner, I just love to cook things for you."

Gunner watched her as she turned and hurried into the kitchen. He had been watching her a lot lately. Once he wondered what she would look like undressed, but he knew she wasn't like the whores. Getting undressed was just for whores. Effy had told him that.

She came back with a tray loaded with the coffee pot, cups and saucers, and pieces of pie neatly placed on small plates. Gunner caught one of the pieces of her cherry pie and took a bite before she could pour his coffee. She watched him gobble down the pie.

"Is it good?" she asked.

Gunner could only nod as he chewed another bite. Effy glowed in the silent praise and poured his coffee. Then she had a bite of the pie. By that time Gunner's large piece was almost gone.

A moment later she watched him take the last bite. "Well, Gunner, you want another piece?"

He nodded. "Yes, please."

"First you have to kiss me." The day before she had explained to him how extremely good friends kissed each other on the lips. She had demonstrated, and he had blinked and then nodded.

"Lips?" he asked.

"Yes, kiss me on my lips." He leaned toward her, and Effy pressed against him with her breasts; when their lips met, she sighed and put her arms around his broad shoulders. Effy held the kiss a long time, and when she let go of him she sighed again.

"Gunner, there's something about kissing that girls like, did you know that? Men don't seem to care so much, but girls really like to be kissed. Of course, kissing can lead to other things, you know what I mean, Gunner?" He shook his head.

Effy caught his hand and pulled it up and pressed it against one of her breasts. "Gunner, sometimes after she's been kissed that way, a girl likes to be felt up here."

Gunner looked at her. She moved his hand so it caressed her breast; then she lifted her hand away but left his at her breast. Gently he rubbed her breast. Effy began to breathe heavily and looked at him with longing in her eyes.

"Gunner, that just feels so wonderful! Do you feel something, too?"

Gunner nodded. "Feels good," he said, his voice almost choking.

She smiled at him and put her hands against his chest. "Gunner, you know that girl, the one who took off her clothes for you?" He nodded. "You remember what you did after that?"

"She took my clothes off, too. I was scared."

"Yes, but you got over that. There's nothing to be scared about with a girl. You know what you did next?"

"Yes." His hand stopped rubbing her breast. She reached up and held it there. "Gunner, that's what married folks do. Mothers and fathers do that, and sometimes it makes babies." She watched him. It was plain to her that what she said was all new to Gunner.

She watched him. Not too fast, she told herself. "Gunner, would you like to reach under my dress and touch my bare breast?"

"That won't make babies?"

"No, Gunner, but you shouldn't tell anyone you did it." She unbuttoned the four fasteners down the front of her blouse and pushed his hand inside. She wore no chemise or wrapper today. His hand found a breast and closed around it. His hand seemed so huge now and her breasts so small.

Gunner rubbed her bare flesh, found her nipple, and squeezed it carefully, then reached for the other breast and did the same. Effy realized she was almost panting. She reached up and kissed Gunner once more on his lips, but only for a brief few

143

seconds; then she caught his hand and took it out of her dress top. She buttoned up her blouse.

"That was very nice, Gunner. I enjoyed your touching me. Did you like it?"

"Yes. I got all hard." He reached to his crotch and rubbed a bulge there that Effy could see. Effy almost jumped up. She calmed herself.

"That's normal, Gunner, especially when two people really enjoy being with each other and like each other as friends."

"You're my friend, Effy," Gunner said with a smile. She glowed. It was the first time she could remember him saying her name. She stood.

"I'll get that pie." She went to the kitchen and brought back the rest of the pie. She put two pieces on Gunner's plate and refilled his coffee cup. He ate the first piece without looking up, then grinned.

"I need to kiss you for this piece of pie," Gunner said. He leaned toward her and touched her shoulder. When he kissed her on the lips, Effy wanted to break out singing. It was the very first sign of affection he had showed.

Yes, yes, it will work, she told herself. Effy sipped her coffee and watched him eating the cherry pie.

"Gunner, I hope you've been thinking about staying here in Flagstaff and helping your mother with the sawmill. There are a lot of things you could do for her. Of course I'll need you to build some new bookshelves for me before long. Have you been thinking about staying?"

Gunner nodded. He finished eating the bite of pie and turned to her. Gently his big hand came out and touched her cheek, then he touched her breast so lightly she hardly felt it.

"I been thinking on it. Might be good to stay here and help Ma. Will you stay here, too?"

"Of course, Gunner. I want to spend lots of time with you. I even have some school books if you want to learn to read. We talked about that one time."

"You'd help me?"

"Of course. I'd be so pleased to help you learn to read. There are so many things I want to show you."

Gunner had finished the pie. He took three big swallows and emptied his coffee cup. He stood abruptly. "I got to go see Ma. She wants me to take something to the mill."

Effy stood too. "A kiss good-bye?" Effy asked.

He looked at her. "Girls sure kiss a lot."

"Girls only kiss men who they like a lot, Gunner Johnson."

She reached up and he bent down and kissed her lips. Then Gunner turned and hurried out the front door without a good-bye.

Effy stood there watching him go. She took two big long breaths and tried to slow her racing heart. Today when he was caressing her breasts, she had almost taken her clothes off. She had surely wanted to. Maybe by the next time he would be ready. Effy knew that she was ready. She had made love only once before, but this time she would be the teacher. She smiled. She could wait. It might take a day or a week, but she could wait for Gunner.

The Professor watched Mace Duncan's house. He and Eagle had harassed the man the night before. Eagle took over the late hours while the Professor slept. Now he was back on duty to see just what the thief did. Would he run? Or would he fight? The Professor figured the man wasn't through battling yet. He had a good thing going; perhaps another killing or two would preserve it.

The Professor saw smoke rising from the chimney when he arrived about six a.m.

An hour later Duncan left the house and walked two blocks away along a row of houses on Main Street. The sawmill manager stopped at one of them and knocked, and a moment later was admitted.

He was inside for about a half hour. When he came out, Duncan headed downtown. Breakfast, the Professor guessed. He went back where he could watch the house Duncan had visited. He wedged in next to an old buggy and an empty house and waited.

The man who came out soon afterward had red hair and a slight build, but he carried a revolver hung low on leather with the end tied down. He must either be a gunman or a man who thought that he was one.

The Professor followed him. The man stopped briefly at the Partridge General Store where he bought a box of .45 rounds; then he went on to the mill. He stowed his six-gun and jacket in a box near where he worked and waited for the mill to begin cutting lumber.

The Professor went to the office and talked to Nancy.

"The redhead down in the yard?" Nancy said in response to his question. "Sure, he's the tallyman. It's an easy job.

Duncan hired him about three months ago. He was from out of town, nobody knows much about him. He's single but doesn't socialize much. His name is Lefty Lewton."

That's when the Professor remembered the redhead carried his iron on the left hip, not the right. "Lefty Lewton. Thanks. We might be making progress." He started to leave. "Oh, don't say anything to Duncan about my being here this morning."

Nancy smiled at him, and he noticed that she had on a pretty dress, one that set off her figure boldly. "Mr. Brown, I wouldn't think of telling him. I still don't like the man. He's been a bit forward to me now and again."

The Professor grinned. "At least he has good taste in pretty women. Oh, what time does the bank open?"

"Usually at nine-thirty."

"Good, I'll see you later."

After the Professor left, Nancy sat at the desk smiling. She primped at her hair and wet her lips so they would be redder. She was right. Nate Brown just might be interested in her!

The Professor had breakfast at a café and waited outside the bank for it to open. The doors unlocked exactly on time, and the narrow-eyed teller smiled at the first few people who came through the door. Then he hurried around the long counter to his teller's window.

There were only two others ahead of the Professor at the cage when he got there. He had waited for the first urgent business people to finish their banking. He was the last customer in line when he stepped up to the window. For just a moment he remembered doing this countless times when he robbed banks. Now he didn't need to do that any more. His anger had burned away, and he had enough cash.

The Professor looked at the name plate over the window. "Mr. Payne, I want five one dollar bills for this fiver. As you do that you listen to me carefully. I have absolute proof that you and Mace Duncan are operating a criminal conspiracy to defraud the Johnson Sawmill out of tens of thousands of dollars.

"Don't be alarmed. I'm not going to tell your employer right now. However I will if you don't agree to tell me exactly how it is done, and then to testify for the prosecution when we bring charges against Mr. Duncan. Do you understand?"

Payne counted out the five one dollar bills with hands that fumbled and had to start over. When the bills were on the counter between them, he nodded slowly.

"I told him it was too good to last. I'll testify only if you swear that I won't be charged with any crime."

The Professor stared at him. "You're in no position to haggle, Payne. I can charge both of you today, and you'll be in the county jail before supper."

Payne looked at the Professor and sighed. He glanced at the bank owner and shivered, then nodded. "All right. He keeps two sets of books. Accounts receivable is cut in half on the big accounts. He works the mail and picks out the checks that he's billed, but not put through the books.

"He cashes those checks for greenbacks here and I get ten percent. That's the whole thing. Simple, if he can keep juggling the books just right. So far nobody but you has caught on. Poor Mrs. Johnson isn't a businesswoman."

The Professor lifted his voice, "Oh, I better have three dollars worth of quarters, too." As the teller counted them out, the Professor made up his mind.

"All right, we have a deal. You stall Duncan on cashing any more checks. Tell him that Mrs. Johnson is checking into her account and that she said Nate Brown was onto some skullduggery. Tell him that and he'll believe it. You understand?"

"I'll try. Duncan is a hard man to deal with."

"Not when he's running scared. After last night he's plenty scared. Remember what I told you, and you might come out of this without going to prison. Oh, of course you'll have to return all of the money you've stolen from the sawmill. About how much is it?"

"You mean my ten percent?"

"Yes."

"Oh my, it's frightening. So far it's slightly over five thousand dollars. I figured it up last night."

"Which means Duncan has stolen over fifty thousand! Payne, I hope you still have all that money." The Professor had been half whispering his words, now he raised his voice. "Well, that about does it. Thank you, Mr. Payne." He turned and walked out of the bank, a determined expression on his face and a firm resolve in his walk.

Chapter Eleven

Bert Filmore paid the man at the gunsmith $11 for the new Colt .45, a well-worn holster, and two boxes of rounds. He had done a lot of shooting in Texas as a boy, but mostly with a rifle. He'd had a six-gun for a while, but it was an old one and it broke. His pa told him they couldn't afford to get it fixed.

He took the weapon out to the edge of town where the canyon narrowed. Bert loaded the Colt and began some target practice. He stood 30 feet away from a foot-thick pine tree and hit it only once out of five tries.

He reloaded and tried again, this time bringing the weapon up to eye height and aiming carefully. Bert hit the tree twice out of the five shots. He kept at it until he had fired 50 rounds, and by then, with slow firing and careful aiming, he could hit the tree four out of five rounds. That would have to be good enough.

He walked back into town from the south and saw a place he hadn't noticed before. The small sign read: "Flagstaff Public Library."

Bert thought it was curious that a little place like this would have a library. He was about to go on past when someone came out and walked directly toward him. The man was huge, close to six-and-a-half feet tall, and on the young side. As soon as he passed, Bert spun around and stared at him.

The man had been big enough and young enough to be Gunner Johnson! He walked into the library and saw the meager collection of books and the homemade shelves against the wall. The woman who sat behind a small desk was more interesting. He went up to her.

Effy smiled. "How may I help you?"

"I thought I saw a friend of mine just leave here. Wasn't that Harry Biltmore who just left?"

The woman frowned and shook her head. "No, I'm afraid you're mistaken. That was Gunner Johnson. His mother owns the Johnson Lumber Mill here in town."

"Oh, well, just goes to show you. I didn't want to walk up and surprise him and find out he wasn't my old friend. Thanks, anyway."

Bert left the library with his heart racing. He looked down the block and could see the big man walking slowly south. He was looking at a team of blacks parked on the street. Bert idled along waiting for the big man. He knew where Eagle stayed, and if he could nail down Gunner he would have a great start. He felt the six-gun at his hip and was glad that he'd taken the target practice.

Gunner tired of looking at the perfectly matched black team and walked across Ponderosa Street and on down Main. He went into the big house on the far corner of the block without knocking, and Bert Filmore grinned widely and headed back to his hotel room. Now all he had to do was figure out how to capture or kill the two men, and then he'd worry about finding the sheriff.

The funeral for Hernando Escobar was that afternoon, and the mill shut down at noon. Almost all of the workers from the mill were at the funeral. There was no Catholic priest in town, and Hernando had not had his last rites, but Mrs. Johnson helped at the funeral, along with the Baptist minister, who said that all men were God's children no matter what branch of Christianity they practiced.

The words of praise were given by three of his co-workers, and then Hernando was lowered into the ground in the pine coffin. Maria and her two boys lingered by the grave; then when the men with the shovels came, the widow turned away sobbing. Juan Romero put his arm around her and helped her walk the three blocks to her house on Ponderosa.

By the time they got there she was through crying. Mrs. Johnson was in the small house and had brought in baskets of food and coffee and all sorts of delightful snacks. Maria sat in her favorite chair and greeted everyone who came to offer one last condolence.

More than 100 people came through the house that afternoon, and the Professor was surprised. Most of the men from the mill came to the funeral and at the post-burial wake. The Professor believed that funerals and wakes and all the trappings were for the living, not for the dead, and in this case, he saw how Maria reacted to the tributes to her dead husband and to the attention she received. It seemed to do a lot to lessen the burden she felt.

Gunner was there, and the Professor dropped by for a few minutes, then left not wanting to have too many of the gang together in the same place. Juan was everywhere, handling the small chores that had to be done. He put out more food, found lost jackets and hats, and thanked everyone at the door as they left.

When the last visitors were gone, Juan, Mrs. Johnson, and Gunner cleaned up the house, then left quietly. Juan lingered and took Maria's hand and told her that if there was anything she needed he would be there to help her. She thanked him and then he too walked into the late afternoon sunshine.

Mrs. Johnson had insisted that Maria and her two sons would move in with her the following day. Maria could do little else. She had no income. And though Hernando had managed to save a little money, it wouldn't last long. And Maria saw that Mrs. Johnson felt so responsible for Hernando's death that she had to take care of the family, or she would carry a great burden of guilt.

On his way back to Main Street, the Professor realized that he hadn't seen Mace Duncan at either the funeral or the wake. It figured the man who had Hernando killed wouldn't have nerve enough to come to the funeral. Mace must not be a very good play actor.

The Professor watched the darkening sky and smiled. Tonight was the second treatment for Mace Duncan and his all-night-terror routine. The Professor stopped by at the Partridge General Store to pick up a few items that he would need. Then he went to the hotel to Eagle's room where he, Eagle, and Willy Boy hashed out the rest of the plot either to terrorize Duncan or to make him so mad that he would lash out and do something stupid. Both outcomes would satisfy the Professor, but he was counting on the murderer doing something stupid.

They began just after dark this time. To get things off with a bang, Eagle lit the fuse to a half-stick of dynamite and threw it near the back porch of the house. It went off with a cracking roar.

A moment later, Mace stepped out and looked around, then fired five shots into the trees behind his house.

Eagle and Willy Boy and the Professor stepped behind large ponderosa pines and grinned at each other. Eagle hurried to the other side of the house and crept up to the blind side, where he began a wild Indian chant that was guaranteed to rout the evil spirits out of a sick warrior. He got it about half done when a shot barked from the front porch, and Eagle faded away into the brush and trees.

They did the door rattling, both front and back door this time, but it brought no outburst from Mace Duncan. They found out why a few minutes later. Duncan came out the front door, locked it, and hurried up the street toward town. Eagle followed him and came back ten minutes later with a report that Duncan was settled into a poker game at the closest gambling saloon and looked set for the night.

"Now we can really get to work," the Professor said. The Professor opened the rear door lock with no problem, and he and Willy Boy crept inside. Eagle stayed out front as lookout.

In the house, the Professor and Willy Boy spread a quart of lard on the sheets in Mace's bed on the side where he slept. They emptied all the kerosene from the two lamps and rolled out the wicks and threw them away. They set up a trap just inside the front door by piling up a washtub, two gallon cans, a can full of nails, and a five-pound bag of flour with the top cut off.

From there they worked toward the back door. Willy Boy laughed softly with each new form of devilment they planted in the house. They found a shotgun in a closet and rigged it with a trip wire. As soon as Duncan came through the door into the kitchen, the shotgun would go off blasting out the kitchen window.

They were ready to do more, but Eagle knocked twice on the kitchen window. Mace Duncan was coming back. They slipped out the back door and hurried into the woods at the side of the house before Duncan could see them.

Mace fumbled a little getting the front door unlocked, then he stepped inside and knocked down the first trap. They heard Duncan screaming. Then all was quiet as they saw the flare of a match, but no blossoming of light from a lamp.

Duncan bellowed in rage again. It was quiet for a moment, and they could see matches flaring one from another as Duncan moved toward the kitchen. They heard Duncan trip over another pile of pots and pans, then get doused with a bucket of water perched on the kitchen door that swung into the living room.

The shotgun blast from the kitchen caught them by surprise, and a minute later Mace Duncan came flying out the rear door, turned for town, and ran as far as he could before he had to stop for breath.

Eagle nodded and followed him. Willy Boy and the Professor looked at the rest of their surprises and shrugged.

"Maybe that's enough for tonight," Willy Boy said.

The Professor grunted. "Yeah, my guess is he won't be staying at home tonight."

Eagle met them as they walked down Main toward the hotel.

"Our friend has taken accommodations at the Flagstaff Hotel," Eagle said. "Fact is, he's right across the hall from my room. Can I get back to work on my chapter now?"

The Professor waved him off, and the other two stood there a minute. "I'm going to try to see if there's a good poker game in town tonight," the Professor said.

Willy Boy waved. "There's a small lady I want to talk to up the street a ways. Maybe you and I can have breakfast in the morning. Unless you're too busy on your crusade."

"It's not a crusade, Willy Boy. I just don't like to see Gunner's ma get her mill stolen right out from under her." He made

160

some marks on the boardwalk with his boot. "You figure that Gunner will stay here now that he's found his ma?"

Willy Boy shrugged. "My bet is that he'll stay. He's got family here, his ma has the biggest business in town and it will probably be his someday. Even hear he's spending a lot of time down at the library."

The Professor chuckled. "Yeah, I was there the first night when his ma sort of threw Effy at Gunner. Seems that the plan is working. They might just make a good couple."

"If he stays here, what happens to our outfit?" Willy Boy asked.

"That would leave four."

"Maybe. Eagle is wrapped up in his books. Odds are that he'll want to go up to Denver and spend all his time working on his writing. He can afford to. Hell, all of us can afford to do anything we want to."

"What about you, Willy Boy? This could be the last mission for the gang. We've worked out the biggest desire of each of us. What will you do now?"

"No question. I still want to find that bastard who gunned down my pa without even asking his name. He's in Texas, or Missouri, or God only knows where. I'll find him and make him die so slow he'll be begging me for a Colt with one round in it."

"Yeah, I know how you feel. But that means we're going to have to start thinking about how we're going to get that money out of San Francisco and divide it."

"Might do that right here after you find your sawmill killer," Willy Boy said. He waved and walked down the street toward a saloon.

The Professor found a game just right for him. He had over $200 in his pocket and went through half of that before he hit a winning streak and came out almost $100 ahead. A hundred dollars to most working men was three month's wages. The Professor kept reminding himself about that.

Working hands on a cattle spread got $25 a month and board and room. A store clerk might make eight dollars a week for six days of work. It made him realize just how much a dollar could buy at the store.

The Professor had one more beer at the bar, then headed for the hotel. He'd had his gear moved to a new spot. On the way in he asked the hotel clerk which room he had now. Number 23. He went up the steps cautiously. No one was waiting for him with a shotgun this time.

He double-checked his room, opening the door and pushing it against the wall, then lighting a match before he looked inside. No one was there. He relaxed for a minute, then stepped in and closed the door.

He pushed a chair under the door handle, threw the bolt, and let his eyes widen to see in the darkness. For a moment he looked out the window at Main Street. The town was winding down. He checked the bed, then lay on top of the covers and relaxed.

Tomorrow he'd push Duncan again. Maybe tomorrow Duncan would crack and his whole scheme come unglued.

Chapter Twelve

For the third day in a row, Gunner's mother gave him two books to take to the library. She smiled when she handed them to him.

"Tell Effy that these are two more books I think she should catalogue and put into her card file and on the shelves. Then see what you can do to help her out around there. She has a lot to do and not much help. We don't have anything to do here until this afternoon when I've ordered two wagons to go over to the Escobar house for the moving. Help us if you want to."

Gunner nodded, put on his hat and went out the door with the two books. It was only a little after eight. The library didn't open for readers to come in until nine. But Effy always let him in early.

She did that morning. She had on a pure white blouse that went from her wrists up to her neck covering her totally. She had tucked the blouse in her skirt at her tiny waist, and the cloth pulled tightly over her breasts.

Gunner handed her the books and said what his mother told him to say, then looked around.

"Anything I can do to help?"

"Yes," Effy said with a smile. "You can help me finish doing dishes. I let them stack up all day yesterday."

Gunner shook his head. "I don't do dishes. That's woman's work."

Effy laughed. "You tell that to my two brothers, both are over six feet and both had to do dishes with me as we all grew up. They still do dishes with their wives. Now come on, I won't let you sneak out of this. You asked what you could do."

Effy laughed and playfully pushed the big man. He pretended to stumble and headed the way she wanted him to go, back through the storeroom to the kitchen.

Effy gave him a dish towel and then handed him a freshly rinsed dinner plate. "Dry it and put it up there on the shelf," she commanded.

Gunner shrugged. "That's easy. I can do that."

A few minutes later they were finished, and Effy carried the dishwater out the back door and threw it in the space behind the library building.

Gunner watched her as she came back. "Pretty," he said.

Effy smiled. "You really think I'm pretty, Gunner? Or are you saying that hoping I have some more cherry pie for you?"

"No, you're a pretty girl."

"Well, thank you, Gunner, let's go in to the other room. We don't have to open the library any special time."

They went into the living room and Effy sat down on the sofa. She pointed to a spot beside her. When Gunner sat down she touched his shoulder.

"Gunner, this pretty girl would like to thank you for helping her with the dishes." She reached up and kissed his lips. Her arms went around him, and his hands came to her shoulders and held her. She let the kiss last a long time.

When she came away she smiled. "You like that, Gunner?"

"Yes. It makes me feel all warm and good, like the way when the girl took off my clothes."

"You enjoyed that, Gunner?"

"I was scared, but I liked it."

Effy kissed him again, let her lips part, and licked his lips with her tongue. Then she pushed hard against him. She picked up his hand and put it over her breast. He rubbed it as he had before and she nodded.

"Yes, Gunner, that makes me feel good." She put her hand on his stomach and then lowered it until she could feel the bulge in his pants behind his fly.

"Are you feeling good?" Effy asked.

He nodded, his eyes wide. "But you said married people did it, nice people who were married beside the whores."

She caught his face with both hands and stared at him. "Yes, Gunner, they do. And sometimes nice people who dearly want to get married do it, just to see if it will work, if they like it."

Gunner grinned. "You want to get married?"

"Yes, Gunner, with all my heart and soul! I've wanted to get married ever since I saw you, since we kissed that first time."

Gunner moved his hand, unbuttoned the white blouse and pushed his hand inside. There was more cloth there, but he went under it until he found her soft, warm breast.

"Now I really feel good," Gunner said. He bent and kissed Effy and she moaned softly with desire.

She unbuttoned the rest of her blouse and let it slide down her arms and took it

167

off. Then she lifted the white chemise that covered her breasts and took it over her head.

Effy sat there bare to the waist, her breasts modest but with large pink areolas and standing tall pink nipples.

"Gunner, about getting married. You think that would be a good idea?"

Gunner held her breasts, one with each hand, and breathed quickly. He nodded.

"Then say it, Gunner. Say it or I'll put my blouse back on and throw you out the front door, and I won't ever let you come back to the library."

Gunner's eyes went wide. "Oh, no. I want to come back."

"Say it about getting married!"

He took a deep breath and shivered. Then Gunner rubbed her breasts gently and nodded. "Yes, Effy. I think it would be a good idea for us to get married."

Effy squealed and reached up and kissed him, then stood and picked up her chemise and blouse and took his hand. "Come on, it's time you saw my bedroom. I want every-thing to be just right the first time for us. Then this afternoon we can tell your mother that we're promised, that very soon we're going to get married!"

Gunner nodded, his grin growing by the

moment as he followed Effy into the bedroom and closed the door.

Juan Romero came with the two big lumber wagons that stopped in front of the Escobar house at one that afternoon. Mrs. Johnson had been there half the morning packing dishes and getting things ready to move. Maria worked beside her tucking away mementos and small treasures.

"You'll have all the room you want in the house," Mrs. Johnson said for at least the third time. "You can use the whole second floor. It's about twice the size of your place here. It's all furnished, but we can move anything you don't want and put your furniture in."

There were four mill hands with each wagon and now they began to carry out furniture and beds and boxes, stacking them on the wagons. Mrs. Johnson saw Juan working with the rest, and she called him over to the side of the house in the shade.

"Juan Romero, I've been watching you. I understand your concern for Mrs. Escobar, but her future is well taken care of." Mrs. Johnson had talked with Gunner when she first met Juan and learned that he was one of the members of the Willy

Boy group. She refused to call them a gang.

"Now I'm wondering about you. I have hopes that Gunner will stay here and help me run the mill. We always need good workers. Have you ever filed saws? It's the third highest paying job in the mill. The job is yours if you want it."

Juan paused and watched the other men loading the wagon. "Mrs. Johnson, I don't think I'd like filing saws at night. But I thank you for the offer. I'm not sure what the rest of the men will be doing. We've been riding together now for more than a year. I'm not sure what I'll be doing either."

Maria came out with a box of her treasures and placed it carefully on the wagon. She looked at them questioningly, then went back to the house.

"Then, too, I've been thinking about Maria and the two *ninos*. Who will take care of them? Who will teach them how to be men?"

Mrs. Johnson lifted her brows and nodded. "She is a beautiful young woman. But you know it would take some time. Her husband is hardly cold in his grave yet."

"I know about this feeling, Mrs. Johnson. I lost my wife not a month ago. It will take some time for me as well, but it is something to think about."

He motioned to the wagon. "I'm not doing my share." He paused. "Did Gunner tell you about the bank in San Francisco?"

"Bank? No. He did say that he had almost fifteen thousand dollars in cash with him. I assumed it was ill-gotten. We put it in the bank here the next day."

Quickly Juan told Mrs. Johnson about the poker game, the winnings, the co-signers on the account and the murder of the member of their gang.

"So, Mrs. Johnson, each of the five of us still has sixty-five thousand dollars waiting for us in San Francisco. All we have to do it go there for the money or send a letter of withdrawal."

"Oh, my! That's a lot of money. He never said a word about it. I wonder why?"

"I'm not sure he totally understood it, but he'll get his share when we draw the money out. What I'm saying is that I'm not exactly destitute, so I could take care of Maria and the boys with what I have now for the rest of our lives."

Mrs. Johnson looked at Juan in a new light.

"Well, I see. Yes, you are in a fine position to do whatever you want to do. I wish you well."

He touched the brim of his hat and hurried out to where the wagons were being crisscrossed with ropes, which tied down the load for the two block trip to Mrs. Johnson's house.

After breakfast that morning, the Professor went by the telegraph office in the railroad station and found three wires waiting for him. He took the figures from the other three large customers down to the mill office, and he and Nancy went to work comparing them with the accounts receivable and the monies received from each one. It took them a half hour before they had the results.

Each of the big customers had paid Johnson Sawmill and Lumber Company more than $6000 in each of the past three months than showed up on the company's income ledger. Each of the firms had its own page and the figures just didn't add up.

"What in the world?" Nancy asked. "I don't understand this, I don't understand it at all."

"Easy, somebody has been stealing at least half of the money that should be going into the company's bank account. Usually a system like this means the thief has to keep two sets of books."

"But there's only one man who has access to the checks and the books and — oh, good Lord!"

"That's the size of it, Nancy; Mace Duncan is the thief. But don't let on that you know. You also realize two men who worked here at the mill have been killed lately. They died because they knew too much."

Nancy's eyes went wide, she started to say something, then her mouth closed and her chin quivered.

"Nancy, just try to relax. There's nothing to be afraid of. Just do your job the way you always do. Leave the fun part of tracking down this villain to me."

Just then Mace Duncan walked into the office. He didn't look as if he had slept much the night before in his hotel bed.

The Professor winked at Nancy, waved at Duncan, and walked out of the office heading for Mrs. Johnson's house. He had the contrasting figures in his pocket.

When he arrived at the Johnson house, the Professor slipped in between the moving men and found Mrs. Johnson in the kitchen making suggestions to the cook for the big dinner she was giving for all of the moving men, their helpers, and the Escobars. "We'll be having three adults and two children for each meal now, Bertha, so I want you to plan your grocery buying accordingly. You'll have twice the budget as before."

The Professor motioned to the tall woman, and she stepped into the parlor with him, then they retreated to the small office she had near the back of the house.

"I have some interesting bank deposit totals for you. I've figured out how Mace Duncan is stealing most of the profits from your business."

"You have proof?"

"Good enough for any court." He showed her the figures for the total checks written by the four large customers, and the totals entered in the accounts receivable ledger.

"I can't believe that Nancy is involved," Mrs. Johnson said.

"No, not Nancy. She didn't know anything about it. Duncan screens the mail, takes out the checks he billed and didn't enter into the accounts receivable, then cashes them at the bank for greenbacks and gold."

"Can we go to the sheriff?"

"We can, but first I'd like to find out what Duncan is doing with the money. He could have a separate account in the bank."

"Mr. Rushmore will tell me if Duncan does. If Duncan had a big account it seems to me Mr. Rushmore would be suspicious. I doubt if he has the money there."

"I'll find it, and then we'll close in on Duncan."

He said good-bye to Mrs. Johnson, warning her not to let on about any of this to Duncan. Then he went back to the hotel and found Willy Boy just getting up.

A half hour later, with Willy Boy serving as his lookout, the Professor went through Duncan's house with a practiced eye, checking every possible spot where the thief could have hidden the cash. But he didn't find it. He even checked the floor boards, and lifted one rug to check under it, but the boards were all nailed down solid.

Since the money wasn't there, the Professor figured it had to be in the mill office. He didn't think Duncan would trust burying the money in the ground. As soon as Duncan left the mill that night, the Professor would give his office and the rest of the big building a complete going-over.

On the way back to the hotel, Willy Boy prodded the Professor. "You going to be with me when I go back to Missouri to find Deeds Conover, that bastard who killed my father?"

"I'm thinking on it. But I've been thinking a lot about San Francisco lately. I liked that town. Then, too, there's that little lady back in Cleveland. Elena Griffen is back there somewhere. When I took her father down in Denver, I didn't mean for it to spill over to her. Yep, I've been thinking more and more about heading that way to find Elena."

"Figures. You were my best hope. From what I see, Gunner will want to stay here. Never can tell about Juan, and Eagle is bursting to keep on working on his damned books."

Willy Boy kicked at the dirt in the street as they crossed to the hotel. "It's all that damn money, it spoiled us. Nobody needs to be wild anymore."

"Hey, I'll be glad to take your sixty-five thousand if it's bothering you so much," the Professor said, a smile edging his face.

Willy Boy laughed. "Hell, it don't bother me that much. I'm just trying to plan for the future here a little."

"First we have to find that money and

nail this damn killer Duncan. Then I'll be a lot more ready to sit down with you and plan things out."

Willy nodded. "Good. Let's get it done then."

Chapter Thirteen

Bert Filmore stood behind a tree near the street not far from the house where Gunner Johnson lived. It was dark. The big moving wagons had left, the dinner was over, and the guests had walked away from the large house. He expected that Gunner would be coming out soon to return to the library. In the afternoon, Bert had observed a budding affair between Gunner and the librarian.

Before long, Gunner came out and walked toward the library down Main Street. As he came to the tree, Bert let him pass, then leaped out behind him and clubbed him on the back of the head with a six-gun. The heavy colt thudded against his skull, and Gunner went down in the dust of the street without a sound.

It took all of Bert's strength to drag Gunner across Main and into the brush and trees behind the school house. There he tied Gunner's hands in front of him with leather thongs, then tied his ankles together.

When he had him safely in the brush, he put a gag around Gunner's mouth so he couldn't scream. Then Bert waited for the big man to come back to consciousness.

Bert squatted there, quivering with delight. He had done it! He had captured the giant and had him at his mercy. Now what should he do? There was no jail in town. The big man had many friends. Where were the other members of the gang?

Bert took out the much-folded wanted poster and read it again. "Wanted: dead or alive — the Willy Boy Gang. Willy Boy Lambier and five members of his gang broke out of the Oak Park, Texas, jail killing two deputies. They later killed eleven members of two posses chasing them.

"A reward of $2,000 is offered for each of the above. Contact Sheriff Jim Dunwoody, Oak Park, Texas."

Bert felt a wild thrill skitter down his backbone. He was staring at a man worth $2,000! It was all so fantastic. Besides this one, he knew where at least one other member of the gang stayed!

Then the reality of his situation crashed down on him. He didn't know if there was a deputy sheriff in town. He had no idea what town the sheriff was in. Most likely, the sheriff would be in the county seat, but where was that in this sparsely settled territory?

He walked down Main to the stores and saloons and began asking people he met if there was a deputy sheriff in town. Most of them shrugged. He went to three saloons and asked the barkeeps. Two said they didn't know. The third lifted a sawed-off, double-barreled shotgun. "This here is the law in my saloon," he said. "We don't need no damn deputy sheriff."

Bert left the saloon shaking his head. He saw the Partridge General Store still open. The owner must know who was sheriff. Bert got there just before Partridge closed up. His question brought a grin to the store owner's face.

"Don't blame you for being confused, young man. See, a new Territory has to be organized into counties. Usually that means that the people make the counties as big as they can, so there don't have to be so many elections to fill the county positions. That's why our county takes in the territory all the way down past Prescott.

"For a while our sheriff was in Phoenix. There's been some talk of splitting the county again and making Flagstaff the county seat, but nothing's been done yet. So we go to Prescott for our sheriff work. It's only about eighty-five miles down there. But the sheriff comes up here every four years just before election day."

"I heard there was a killing recently," Bert said. "Don't the sheriff come up to investigate murders?"

"Not usually. See our sheriff is more an office man; he doesn't have many deputies he trusts, and he can't ride a horse, so he just passes on most things."

Bert shook his head, and went out of the store. He marched to the hotel. By damn! he'd take Gunner back to Texas on the train if he had to. That shouldn't be too hard. He'd use the manacles he had brought, fit them on Gunner tight, wake him up, and march him down to the station before sunrise. Then he'd get Gunner on the train heading east. As he remembered, the train left about seven o'clock. There'd be no time for his gang members to even know Gunner was missing.

Yes, with a little luck it just might work. As soon as he came to the first good-sized town with a sheriff down the tracks, he'd have the sheriff wire to Dunwoody about the capture. Bert decided he'd pick up some leg irons and a sawed-off shotgun just to make sure he got Johnson to Texas. Yeah! it would work.

The Professor moved into the mill office as soon as he saw Mace Duncan leave. Willy Boy followed the mill manager and came back and told the Professor that Duncan had settled in at a café for his supper.

They checked all the usual hiding spots: behind cabinets, on the bottom of drawers, in closets, behind old records. They worked for an hour and found nothing, always careful to leave the spot searched in the same condition they had found it.

Willy Boy ran back to the café and found Duncan just leaving, heading for his house this time. He stayed there only long enough to get a bag of items and returned downtown to the hotel.

"Looks like we have all night if we need it," Willy Boy said when he slipped back into the mill office.

The Professor had checked with the night watchman, so he knew the Professor and Willy Boy were there. They sat on a desk outside of Duncan's office.

"Damn, I keep wondering where I'd hide fifty or sixty thousand dollars in cash," the Professor said. "All the places I thought of weren't the ones Duncan must use. Where does he have it stashed?"

They worked again, trying every possible spot where a cardboard box could be placed with a lot of money in it. About ten o'clock they gave up and headed downtown.

Juan ran up to them, his eyes wary and his face strained and angry. "Gunner is missing. His mother said he went to the library tonight. He always gets home by nine. I was there about nine-thirty, so his mother asked me to check at the library. It was dark and the librarian came to the door and said Gunner hadn't been there tonight at all. He left the house about six-thirty."

"Trouble," Willy Boy said. "Gunner wouldn't just vanish. If he said he'd be home by nine, you could bet your last two cents he'd be there. You suppose that Deputy Seth Andrews from Oak Park, Texas, is in town?"

Juan shook his head. "I think he was too hurt and used up after Denver to ever chase us again."

"Any of you been aware of being followed or stared at during the last couple of days?" the Professor asked. None of the others indicated they had. "I thought one guy was staring at me when I was playing poker one night. But then I lost and he lost interest in me. Maybe he was going to waylay me soon as I got outside with my winnings."

"So what can we do?" Willy Boy asked.

"Get Eagle and a lantern. He might be able to track Gunner for a ways in the dust of the street. There isn't a lot of traffic after dark around here."

A half hour later Eagle found Gunner's tracks leading away from the three-story Johnson house. They were hard to miss with Gunner's size 12 boots. They followed his trail a quarter of a block; then they found that the dust was all scrambled and marked up near a tall ponderosa that still stood at the edge of the street.

"Looks like a bunch of chickens have been scratching through here," Juan said.

Eagle shook his head. "Gunner fell down." He moved the lantern over a few feet and found what he was afraid he might.

"See the two trails in the dust? Somebody dragged somebody else across the street to that brush." The four men drew their six-guns and charged the brush on the other side of the road. Even Eagle with the lantern had a hard time working into and through the brush.

They trampled it from one side to the other, from the house down to the school-house yard, but nowhere did they find Gunner or any indication that he'd been there.

Eagle went back and looked again where the drag marks went into the brush. He moved in as far as the heel marks went, and there he put down the lantern and studied each piece of grass, each weed and small plant.

Soon he outlined a long narrow section. "Gunner was here. He lay in this spot for some time, maybe an hour or more." He pointed just beyond. "Later he came back to consciousness and stood and walked away through the brush toward First Street, the street a block over to the left. Let's see what we can find over there."

It took Eagle almost a half hour working back and forth across First Street before he found the footprints. First Street was mostly fronted by houses and tents and the Baptist Church on this end. There were no boardwalks.

Gunner had to have walked in the street and along various placed in the soft dirt and dust; he had left prints that were easy for Eagle to read.

"He's being led or pushed by someone. His steps are uneven and short compared to those he usually takes. There is another set of much smaller prints on the left side of Gunner. That suggests to me that someone had a gun in Gunner's left side. The gun was held by a right-handed person."

Eagle kept walking, swinging the lantern back and forth. A man walking toward them asked what they were doing, and Eagle told them he was trying to track a runaway horse. The man moved on.

Half way up the block three large tents were lighted brightly by lanterns and lamps, and men and women shouted and sang and roamed around the street.

"Best whorehouse in town," Willy Boy said.

They followed Gunner's trail another 20 feet and Eagle shook his head. "Too many boots and shoes have been walking along here. I've lost the tracks." He motioned and they walked to the far side of the three tents that were the portable fancy house, and there Eagle began to search again for the tracks. But he couldn't find them. Eagle went back and forth across the street several times but at last shook his head.

"Just can't find them. Somebody's got

Gunner and brought him down here some-where, but I don't know why."

The Professor walked another tent up and looked past it. "If the guy who has Gunner is a bounty hunter, why isn't he trying for all of us? Or does he just want to take one of us and run? Right over there is the end of the train tracks and the station for the Atlantic and Pacific railroad."

"There isn't a sheriff in town for him to deposit Gunner with while he looked for the rest of us," Willy Boy said. "No way he could shoot down Gunner and get a sheriff to wire Texas with a go-ahead on the bounty payment."

Eagle snorted. "So he marches Gunner down here at night planning to get on the train as soon as it gets here in the morn-ing."

The Professor eyed the tents and four houses. "He could be in any of these places. We could tear them apart one by one until we found him. But it'll be easier to stand guard along here until morning and catch him when he tries to get him to the train. Find your spots. We'll sleep now and be up by four a.m. I'll stand the first watch. Who wants the second one?"

Eagle held up his hand. Two of the men found spots to lie down behind the tents within sight of the rails. Willy Boy perched beside one of the frame houses with a good view of the street. The Professor paced up and down the street watching everyone and everything that moved. He would be on duty until one a.m. Then he'd wake Eagle. By four in the morning, all four of them would be hiding, awake and watching for anybody trying to move Gunner to the train.

Nothing happened besides a lot of yelling at the whorehouse before it was time for the Professor to wake Eagle. The Indian was up before the Professor got within 20 feet of him, his six-gun aimed dead center on the other man.

"Hey, easy with the iron," the Professor growled. Eagle grinned in the darkness and moved out where he could see the street, especially the tents. At least three of them were transient hotels that charged 20 cents a night.

Eagle kept his lookout from three vantage points, but by four a.m. nothing had changed. He went around cautiously waking up the other three men, then they selected new hiding spots where they wouldn't be conspicuous during the morning hours, and the four waited for dawn and the chance of finding Gunner — and the bounty hunter who had captured him.

Chapter Fourteen

Mace Duncan lay in his hotel room and watched the first traces of light break into the dawn sky. He'd had a good night's sleep, but now what did he do? He was sure by this time that whoever was after him was watching every move he made.

That damned Nate Brown! He had probably explained to Mrs. Johnson why there was such a low profit on the mill. But they had to have proof of Duncan's thievery; no one could prove it! He thought again: the one man who knew anything was the teller at the bank, Warner Payne. Yes, he had become a definite liability.

Duncan got to his feet, dressed quickly, and left the hotel by the side door without even the clerk at the desk seeing him. He carried a derringer in his pocket and a knife in his boot. He knew where Warner Payne lived. The young man was a bachelor who had expensive tastes in women. Duncan knew he used all of his money entertaining the best whores in town. Duncan hoped he was at home that morning.

It was not quite full light yet when Duncan came to the back door of the small house where Payne lived. He slipped in the unlocked door and looked around Payne's kitchen. Beyond that were a living room and two doors opening off it. He checked one door and found a storeroom.

Behind the other door Warner Payne lay on his bed under a sheet. He was alone. Duncan decided not to use the knife. He lifted the .45 caliber two-shot derringer and placed it over Payne's heart.

The man came awake with a jolt, causing the weapon to move off center as Duncan pulled the trigger. The round slammed through Warner Payne's chest above and to the side of his heart, barely nicking his lung.

The bank clerk wailed in anger and pain. "Who in hell are you?" he yelled. "Why do you want to kill me?"

Duncan backhanded him with his left hand slapping him back to the bed, and Payne stared up in amazement, recognizing his assailant.

"Duncan? Mace Duncan. I thought we were partners. Haven't I been cashing your checks?"

"You have, but you might have told someone."

"Christ no! I swore a vow of silence, remember? We made a deal. I get ten percent and I don't ever tell anybody!"

"I remember, but the threat of a prison term would make you break that vow in a hurry. I can't take that chance."

Duncan lifted the little pistol again, and Payne surged up and lunged at him. The derringer exploded a second time; this round was aimed better. The heavy round slammed into Payne's chest, shattered the left half of his heart, and Payne slumped, still grasping for Duncan as he died.

Duncan didn't pause to look at the body. He retraced his steps through the small house, looked out the back door but saw no one, so he slipped out, closed the door, and faded into the first light of dawn. He walked through the block to First Street, then north toward the mill and his own rented house. One last loose end had been snipped off. What else did he have to do to protect himself?

The only chance to get away from town without being tracked was by stage toward California, because there was no telegraph in that direction yet. But he would have to use a disguise. He was sure that Mrs.

Johnson would have someone watching every stage and every train out of town. He'd have to go soon, that day, or the next at the latest.

He'd have to get the money together quickly. He knew that somebody had searched his desk and his office. Probably that damned Nate Brown. But he couldn't have found a thing because none of the cash was there. Duncan had hidden it all right under their noses.

He had $10,000 in a special Mill account that he had opened several months earlier, and none of the money showed up on the regular bank statement. The statement for the special account was mailed to him personally. He controlled it, and Mrs. Johnson didn't know about it even though it wasn't in Duncan's name.

Besides the money in the special account, he had put $20,000 in the box marked old records that he'd given to Nancy to seal up and file in her small closet. If Brown had looked out there, Nancy would have vouched for that box. The money was spaced among the old records in bundles of $100 bills so they hardly made a bulge. There was ten bundles in all, each with 20 bills.

He'd even have Nancy bring it to his office. He had breakfast at the Flagstaff Restaurant and was feeling better. It didn't bother him a whit that he had killed a man that morning. It had to be done. He knew that Payne was a part of the scheme that had to be eliminated sooner or later. And Brown had forced his hand.

There was a stage out of town about four that afternoon. He'd have his disguise on, one small suitcase, and the money. He'd get his ticket early in order to avoid raising suspicion.

As soon as he got to the office, he asked Nancy to bring him that last box of records that he asked her to seal and store for him. He had to verify that a check had been paid by finding the actual draft.

"I can do that, Mr. Duncan."

"Actually this is one I need to look up myself. It could have been my mistake and I want to correct it."

She smiled. "Yes, sir. I know right where that box is. We really need a better filing system for our older records. I'll see what I can figure out."

Ten minutes later, he had the box, snapped the lock on the inside of his office door, and cut open the sealing tape that Nancy had used on the box.

He found the ten bundles of $100 bills

exactly where he had placed them. He took them out, replaced the folders and pushed the bills into an envelope. Twenty thousand dollars right there in his hands! That was more money than 90 percent of working men ever saw in their lives.

A half hour later he took a large screwdriver from his desk, pocketed it, and went out the back door to the privy. It was a two holer and sat 50 feet downhill from the office. He went inside, locked the door, stood on the bench, and reached high on the slanted inside top of the outhouse.

There under a board that had been nailed to the side, he pulled out a bundle wrapped in oil cloth and held with string. His nervous fingers fumbled as he untied the string. Yes! Inside was another $20,000. He pushed the package in his pocket, dropped the screwdriver into the open hole, and walked back into the office.

Duncan initialed some bills to be paid by Nancy, then took care of filling an order for Texas before he saw that it was after ten o'clock and time to go to the bank. He realized that he was a walking gold mine as he went down to the bank with the company's regular deposit. He saw a commotion outside the bank and heard the news.

The teller, Warner Payne, hadn't come

to work that morning, and the banker found him dead, murdered in his bed. Duncan nodded at the news and went inside. There were three people in line. The banker himself, H. L. Rushmore, was working one of the teller windows and the bookkeeper the other one.

Duncan drew the banker's window and presented a check to close out the special Jackson Lumber Mill back order account. The banker hesitated.

"Can we just transfer this into the other mill account?" Rushmore asked.

"It's a cash matter, I'm afraid. Some men are in town who won't accept a check. You know how it is."

"That's going to run me short on cash, but I guess I can do it. I have some five-hundred-dollar bills, will they do?"

"Hundreds would be better," Duncan said. The banker came back quickly and quietly counted out the ten stacks of hundreds for Duncan.

"Most of this will be coming back to the bank in the next few days, but these men insist on cash, even though they will pay cash for lumber orders day after tomorrow. Some people are crazy."

Duncan was out of the bank before Rushmore remembered his talk with Mrs.

Johnson. This hadn't been Duncan's money, it was mill money in a mill account. He wondered if he should tell her anyway. He decided he would if she came in that day.

Duncan hurried back toward his house. He had no reason now to go back to the mill. He needed his disguise and a ticket on the stage that left about four that afternoon.

The four members of the Willy Boy Gang watched everything as the dawn brightened into day. So far they had seen no one who looked suspicious or who had Gunner Johnson in tow.

The Professor figured whoever it was would have Gunner's hands tied, but how would the man get Gunner on board quietly? The Professor hoped they'd see Gunner coming stumbling out of the whorehouse tents, but he didn't think that they would.

They waited until nearly six o'clock, and by then more people moved on the street. Later a stream of men filed toward the mill well in advance of its seven o'clock starting whistle. About the time the whistle blew, the train would leave town.

The Professor could see the train tracks now and the people waiting for the incoming train. It would be there for about an hour before it made the turn around on the circle track and headed back for points east.

At six-fifteen the Professor saw a man come out of one of the tent houses and direct some others. Two men came out with a house door. On the door lay a man swathed in bandages. His face was almost covered, and his hands were bound at his sides. He had been tied on the door so he wouldn't roll off.

The two big men carried the door down the middle of the street. The other man walked in front waving wagons and rigs and buggies aside as he guided the men 50 feet down First Street, then between the houses at an alley that went directly to the end of the railroad tracks and the small station.

Willy Boy strolled out from his hiding spot and angled toward the improvised stretcher. He glanced at the man on the door, then at the man in front.

"Looks busted up bad," Willy Boy asked. "What happened to him?"

"Didn't you hear? Logging accident," the tall slight man in the lead said. "A log crushed his legs and arms, smashed in his face. We're going to get him on the train and to the hospital over at Albuquerque."

Willy Boy shrugged and walked away.

The Professor heard part of the exchange. How would a kidnapper get Gunner on board a train without his making a big explosive scene and break up some bodies? Why not tie him down on a door and pretend he was sick?

The Professor hurried toward the men with stretchers at an angle so he could intercept them. He stood solidly in front of the man indicating he wouldn't move. The slender man leading the stretcher stopped.

"Yes?" he asked.

"I'm Sheriff Morgan, I don't recall any bad accident in the woods. You sure that man is going for medical attention?"

"Absolutely. I'm Doctor James Lincoln, I came in on the train yesterday. I'm working with the Johnson Mill folks. Ask them about the accident. Now we really must get to the train. It's arriving now, and they said I'd have to be there early to get the stretcher on board."

"Oh, in that case, I'll be glad to help." The Professor motioned and the other three men in the gang rushed over. Willy Boy walked beside the man who said he was a doctor.

"Let's set the door down on the edge of

the platform here, Doctor Lincoln," the Professor said. "I'd like a word or two with your patient."

As the Professor said it, Willy Boy crowded the doctor against the platform, gently lifted his six-gun from his holster, and pushed it against the man's side.

"Doctor, no one can see this weapon. So you just be good and stay put while we check our patient. Otherwise you're a dead man, understand?"

Bert Filmore nodded. Sweat ran down into his eyes. He had recognized Eagle at once as soon as he came up. He figured the tall man was the Professor. The small guy would be Willy Boy himself, and the Mexican had to be Juan Romero. They were all right here breathing on him, and he didn't even have his gun!

The Professor used his knife and sliced some of the inch-wide gauze strips from across the man's face. After half a dozen were removed, they all saw Gunner's eyes blinking desperately at them. He tried to say something, but a gag restricted him. The Professor cut it away and Gunner bellowed in rage.

"Damn bastard slugged me from behind. He tied me up!"

The two men who had been carrying the

stretcher took off at a run, but the Willy Boy Gang let them go. It took them about five minutes to get Gunner untied and unstrapped from the door; then they found the key to the manacles on his hands and freed him.

Gunner shook his hands until the circulation came back in them. He stamped his feet a minute, then pushed in where Willy Boy held Bert Filmore under his six-gun.

Gunner slammed one big fist into Bert's jaw jolting him to the side. Willy Boy grinned and stepped back. Gunner knocked the man down four times, and the last time he didn't get up.

The Professor knelt beside the man and shook his head to bring him back to the land of the regretful.

"What's your name?" the Professor asked.

"Filmore, Bert Filmore."

"You're from Oak Park, Texas?"

The man's eyes flared. "Yes. And the five of you killed my pa a year and a half ago when you broke out of jail."

"That was his fight, not yours. You after revenge or just the reward?"

"First I wanted to kill you all."

"Not a chance. Give us one good reason why we shouldn't just kill you now and be done with it?"

"You've changed. All of you. You're not the same men you were when you broke out. You can't kill as easy now as you did then."

"I can. Want me to prove it?" Willy Boy asked, lifting the six-gun so it aimed at Bert's face.

"You're Willy Boy," Bert said. "No, I don't want you to prove it."

"What are we going to do with you?" the Professor asked.

"Leave him just enough money to buy a ticket to Albuquerque," Eagle said. "That way he won't be coming back here."

Romero nodded. The Professor looked at Willy Boy who shrugged. Gunner was still too mad to vote. The Professor took a purse from Bert and checked the cash. He had $40. Willy Boy took a double gold eagle and went to get a one way ticket to the New Mexico town. He came back with a dollar in change and gave it to Filmore.

"We'll stay with you until you get on the train and it leaves," the Professor said. "You try to get off and you eat lead, understand?"

"My suitcase, my things at the hotel —" Bert began. He stopped.

"You're lucky to be getting out of town without a few bullet holes in your skin,"

Eagle said. "Go back to Texas and forget about vengeance, find a little girl and settle down."

Willy Boy unstrapped the gun belt from the Texan, shoved the six-gun in leather, and slung the belt over his own shoulder.

"Eagle, you want to shepherd this young man to the train?" the Professor asked.

Eagle nodded, took the ticket from Willy Boy, and nudged Bert Filmore toward the station. The train was starting to load passengers, so they got on the last car.

Eagle waited with the man, who sat in a seat and scowled.

"Filmore, you're a lucky bastard, remember that. Six months ago if we'd run into you, you'd have been buzzard bait by this time. You stay on the damn train and go back to Texas."

As the train began to move, Eagle ran to the door and jumped off. He made sure the ex-bounty hunter was still looking out the window when the train made it's circle and came back heading engine first down the tracks to the east.

Chapter Fifteen

Eagle ran to Mrs. Johnson's house to tell her the good news about finding Gunner. Effy was there too, and both women had been crying. When they heard Eagle's news, they dried their tears. Effy splashed water on her face to reduce the puffiness, and both went out in the front yard to meet Gunner upon his return.

He came with part of the white gauze wrapping still on him. He broke into a run when he was 20 yards away and went first to Effy, picking her up and whirling her around and kissing her. His mother looked pleased.

When he stopped turning, his mother hugged him as well, and the three walked into the house. The rest of the Willy Boy Gang faded away. Eagle was anxious to get back to his writing. Willy Boy and the Professor figured they could have a long morning nap. Juan went to the back door of the Johnson house hoping that Maria might be there.

Inside the house, Gunner told his mother and Effy what had happened to him. They listened and Effy held his hand.

"Then the guys came and figured out what was going on. Willy Boy got the bounty hunter's gun and then it was all over. He's on the train heading back to Texas."

As Gunner talked, Mrs. Johnson fixed him breakfast. She fried six eggs, made a skillet full of country fried potatoes, toasted three slices of bread on the hot stove top, and set a pint-sized mug of coffee in front of him.

He ate and looked for more when he finished. Mrs. Johnson brought out a double-sized helping of oatmeal she had cooked. Gunner grinned.

"You sure remember what I like," Gunner said. He caught Effy's hand. "You got to tell it all to Effy, because she and I are going to get married."

Mrs. Johnson let out a small cry of joy and hugged Gunner and Effy. The women exchanged secret glances; then they began to plan the wedding.

"I want to stay here, Ma, and help you with the mill. I can do some things down there. We'll figure out what's best. Effy can help decide."

Maria's two little boys ran through the kitchen. Maria looked in and said she was sorry and herded her sons up the steps to the second floor.

"You'll stay here, of course," Mrs. Johnson said. Effy shook her head. "No, we decided that we'd stay behind the library until we can get a house. We don't need anything near this big. Something with about three bedrooms. We'll look around."

Mrs. Johnson had frozen when Effy said no. Now she tried to smile. "Yes, Effy, I guess that would be best. I'd want a place of my own if I was just starting out. Fine, we'll buy whatever you want or build you a new house. Heaven knows we have all the lumber we need." They all laughed.

"Gunner, why don't you show Effy your room up on the third floor. You kids can talk about the wedding, too."

Gunner grabbed Effy's hand and headed for the living room door. Effy looked back at Mrs. Johnson, who grinned and nodded. Effy winked at her future mother-in-law, as she and Gunner hurried up to the third floor.

Gunner's large bedroom had a view over the town, which pleased Effy. She smiled at Gunner and said, "It's a fine room, Gunner. Let's sit on the bed and talk."

They sat down and Effy kissed Gunner at once and then pulled him with her back on the bed. She kissed him a dozen times and felt him stirring.

"Right now, Gunner! Please make me feel all warm and wonderful right now!" She moved from under him, ran to the door and quietly threw a bolt locking it, then opened the buttons on her blouse as she returned to the bed.

"Last night I thought I might never see you again. Now I want to make love to you every chance I get."

Gunner reached out for her and nodded. Then he helped her take off her blouse.

Downstairs, Juan knocked on the back door and Maria answered. When she saw Juan, she went outside and sat down on the steps. She looked at him. He was unshaven, his hair all rumpled and snarled from the night's work, and he looked tired. Still he smiled at her.

Maria put a small frown on her pretty face. "Juan Romero, you do not need to feel sorry for me or worry about me. I can take care of myself. I have a patron who will care for me and my boys. You are free to go on your wandering ways."

Juan watched her. Maria sat straight, her

head held high and stiff, her face fixed, but the frown soon faded. Her shoulders were back and her breasts forward. For a moment she seemed frozen; then slowly she turned toward him.

"I am not a forward person, Juan Romero. I am in mourning for my husband. It is not proper for you to be calling on me this way."

"I know. But these are difficult times and we are in a strange land, and somehow I had a feeling that I should help and protect you."

"That is kind of you, Mr. Romero." Maria stopped. Her shoulders, which had begun to relax, came back stiff and straight again. "Perhaps —" Maria sighed. "This is so hard. I never thought it would be so hard."

Maria collapsed and sagged against him. Juan's arms went around her, and she cried silently against his shoulder.

"I miss Hernando so much! I can't eat. I see him in everything the boys do and every time they speak. He is still here, yet he is gone. Sometimes I think I'll go out of my mind."

Juan smoothed her long black hair and patted her shoulder. Holding her tightly, he didn't say a word.

She finally finished crying and leaned away from Juan to wipe her eyes.

"I'm sorry that I had to cry. I'm usually a stronger woman than that."

Maria looked up at Juan, her big brown eyes filled with worry and wonder and loss. For just a moment she almost cried again, but she blinked back the tears and shook her head.

"I told myself that I had cried enough." She edged away from him so they didn't touch. "I guess that you will be moving on with the others soon."

"I don't know. Gunner told us that he is going to stay here. He's going to marry Effy."

Maria flashed a beautiful smile despite her own sadness. "Oh, that is so good. She's a fine person and they will be happy." The word made her look away suddenly. Juan put his arm around her and felt her tighten up.

"As a friend, Maria. I'm comforting you as a friend."

Maria tensed again, then relaxed. "I'm so miserable with Hernando gone that sometimes I want to die!"

"Don't say that. You have good friends. I'll be here to help you any way that I can." He lifted her chin so he could see her face.

"Maria, I'm going to stay. If the others leave, that's fine. I won't be going with them. The bunch is broken up anyway, I think. I want to stay. I want to be near you."

"Mr. Romero, that is highly improper. I'm a new widow. You shouldn't even be thinking about anything like that."

"I'm sorry. I want to be a friend. Right now that's all, just a friend."

Maria relaxed a little.

"It isn't like we were in a Mexican village where we had traditions to maintain. We are here, alone."

Maria sighed. She looked at the distant hills and shook her head. "I can remember my wedding day so clearly. It was only six years ago. We lived in a small Texas town near the border. My marriage was arranged. I had never even seen Hernando until the day I met him at the church altar. I was so frightened I could hardly walk."

"But it became a love match?"

"Yes. He was so kind and gentle, and so handsome! I was the luckiest of women. Now I'm the most unlucky."

"I shall try to change your luck, Maria. Change it back to good luck."

"Perhaps in a year."

"I'll be here, Maria, waiting, helping,

watching. Anything I can do for you, I'll be more than willing."

Maria looked up at him, her large brown eyes brimming with tears again. "Juan, I know you are fine and gentle and caring. If you can wait for a year, I will know that you are true, and then we will talk. Until then, I can't touch you." She moved away.

Juan nodded. "In Mexico it would be a year. Here we are in a different society; here things are not the same. I think a mourning time of six months would be plenty."

Maria frowned, then lifted dark brows. "As you say, Juan, it is different here. Six months it is." She smiled and moved away from him an inch more. "Even if we can't touch, we can talk. I would hope that you might be a friend I can talk to often about the boys, about Mexico, about how to teach my sons to be good Mexican men."

"I would be honored, Maria."

She stood without letting him help her. "I feel a lot better, Juan Romero. I like the sound of your name more and more. I'll look forward to seeing you again."

That afternoon, Juan bought the small house where Maria used to live. He paid cash, $900, and put nearly $12,000 in the local bank. Mr. Rushmore was surprised at the amount and at receiving it all in cash. He counted it twice, then entered the figures in a passbook for a checking account and smiled.

"It's good doing business with you, Mr. Romero," the banker said as Juan left the bank. And Juan knew it was the first time Rushmore had ever been nice to a Mexican.

Juan spent the rest of the afternoon buying furniture for his house and getting it hauled to the place. He checked out of the hotel and bought a big bag of groceries at the Partridge General Store, then walked home.

Maria paced up and down in front of the small house. She was surprised when she saw him coming up the sidewalk.

"Oh! I wondered who had moved in here."

"I bought the house," Juan told her.

"Oh, my! Then you really are staying."

"Yes, shortly after six months have passed, I hope to take a wife."

Maria looked up sharply, then smiled. "At first I thought you were being too forward. Of course, a man can take a wife anytime he finds a good woman who will have him."

"I hope that won't be a problem."

"In six months it will be no problem." Maria watched him a moment longer, then a special smile lit her face, and she turned and walked away from him around the block to the Johnson's big house.

"This is going to be the longest six months of my life," Juan told himself. He set his jaw and carried the food inside and began stocking the shelves.

Mace Duncan took a deep breath, then with a pair of scissors cut off as much of his full beard as he could. He snipped and snipped, then used a straight razor to shave his dark beard and thick moustache. It had been five years since he had been clean shaven, and he hardly recognized himself when he looked in the mirror. Yes, he looked different, but not different enough. He took the scissors and comb and cut his own hair. He usually trimmed it every two weeks. Now he cut it severely so it was about half the thickness as usual, and he combed it down well to one side.

Yes, he nodded at his reflection, that would help. He found the old horned-rim glasses he used to wear for reading and put them on. From his suitcase he found an old hat. It was a wide-brimmed one that he could pull low over his eyes. He tried it on and saw instantly that there wasn't one man in a thousand who would recognize him with a quick look. The only thing that might give him away was his height, but he could do nothing about that, except slump a little.

The clock showed nearly noon. He selected what he wanted to take with him and put it all in one small suitcase. He wasn't taking more luggage because he could buy whatever he needed down the line. But he did need one bag so he would seem like the other passengers and not attract attention.

He avoided wearing one of his black suits; instead he picked out a well-worn jacket and pair of pants that didn't match. Duncan put on a pair of old shoes and checked the mirror again. He looked nothing like the well-dressed manager of the big mill. Now he was just another poor man moving west.

Mace carried all of the money on him. Two of the packets went into his jacket pockets. The third he divided between the front pockets of his pants. It was a bit bulky, but what a wonderful way to feel fat!

Just after one o'clock, he left the small house by the back door, walked half a block over and then down Sawmill Street to Main. The California Stage Company had its depot just below the livery on Main Street. There were no other customers at the window when Duncan asked for a ticket to Los Angeles.

"Having a little trouble getting through the mountains, but shouldn't be snowed in yet. You'll make it," the ticket clerk told Mace when he asked about the condition of the trail.

Duncan paid the fee, took his ticket, and used a strange voice to ask about the time.

"Stage should be here about 3:30 and pull out promptly at 4 p.m. There's a pretty fair café next door in case you want to feed up before you leave."

Duncan had seen the ticket agent around town many times, but he didn't seem to recognize his customer. Duncan went next door and left his hat on as he ate at a back table. He had a steak with all the side dishes. Knowing stagecoach-stop cooking, it might be some time before he had another really good meal.

He spent more than an hour over the food, taking a second slice of cherry pie, then sat on the bench outside the depot waiting for the stage. Two women came and sat down by him each with a suitcase. He didn't know them. A woman with two children arrived, but they were just seeing off one of the women. He breathed easier since no one seemed to know he was leaving town.

The stage rolled in ten minutes early, and Duncan gave a long sigh. He was worried it might have been wrecked or held up somewhere back across the state.

Six men and women got down from the stage and retrieved their luggage before hurrying off to their destinations. The driver came out of the café and threw his three new passenger's bags on top or in the boot. He tied everything down. Duncan watched as the stable boys unhooked the team of six, drove them away, then brought over a new team of six in less than two minutes.

The rig was one of the big, heavy Concord stagecoaches with the leather through braces that had some degree of shock absorbing ability. Veteran coach riders said it also set the coach into a gentle swaying pattern much like that of a ship at sea.

Before the stage left, a cowboy with saddle and carpetbag came with a ticket in hand. The new driver came out and took over. Since this was the end of the line, there was a change of drivers. The new driver growled as he untied the gear on top, then lashed down the cowboy's luggage, and jumped on the high seat out front. When the cowboy asked if he could ride beside him, the teamster grunted, pleased. It wasn't often he had company on the high seat.

A minute until 4 p.m. the big Concord lunged forward, and the horses paced outward. Duncan had claimed a window seat early on, and now he had his back to the seat and watched out the window as the small town of Flagstaff faded out of sight.

The California Trail was not the best stage road in the world, and they probably would average less than four miles an hour, but that was almost 100 miles a day. Duncan knew all that and accepted it, because he had $50,000 in his pockets and was on his way to a new life as a rich man!

Back in Flagstaff, the Professor came awake from his small nap about two in the afternoon. He stopped by for Eagle, and they went down to the hotel dining room. Juan found them there and told them about buying the house.

"So you're staying here," the Professor said. "That's three out of the original six. We're falling apart."

"Bound to happen sooner or later,"

216

Eagle said. "I'll be moving on to Denver when this is all over."

"Moving on," the Professor said. "I wonder what our man Duncan is doing this afternoon. We haven't harassed him at all today."

As the men spoke, Nancy came in the dining room and looked around. When she spotted the Professor, she walked straight to his table.

"Mr. Brown, you said to tell you if Mr. Duncan did anything unusual. He has."

The Professor introduced Nancy to the men at the table. Then he asked, "What did he do?"

"He took the deposit to the bank this morning as usual, but he never came back. I checked with the bank, and they said he had been there and made a substantial withdrawal."

"How much?"

"Ten thousand dollars."

The Professor came to his feet quickly. "He's running. How can he get out of town?"

"The train left early this morning," Eagle said. "We saw it. He couldn't have been on it. That's the only train out today."

"The stage heads west about four this

afternoon," Nancy said, "that's not for almost an hour yet."

The Professor rubbed his face with one hand. "Eagle, you know where his house is. Go out and check it to see if it looks like he's running. I'll check near the stagecoach depot to see if he's buying a ticket. That would be the best time to stop him. I hope he's not waiting somewhere and planning to get the morning train out.

"Juan, you go back to the mill with Nancy and see if Duncan left any clues in his office. We better move. The stage might decide to leave early."

The Professor walked quickly down Main Street. He had seen the California Stage Company depot at the end of the street near Mill Street. As he crossed over on the other side of the dirt avenue, he saw that the stage wasn't in yet. When it came in, it would stop right in front and get fresh horses from the livery.

The Professor settled down in a wooden chair in front of the Four Aces Saloon across from the depot and waited. He could see the bench in front of the depot. Two women sat there on one end, and on the other end a man seemed to be sleeping. He held a suitcase protectively between his legs, and he stretched out on the bench

218

with his head against the wall. He had worn shoes, and his clothes looked old.

The man's clothes were certainly not a traveling outfit for the snappy-dressing Mace Duncan. The man moved and the Professor saw the sun glint off the man's clean-shaven jaw and face. The Professor dismissed him since Duncan had a full black beard. Besides, Duncan wouldn't sit out in the open waiting for the stage if he was running away with $10,000. Duncan would probably stay in the café or the depot itself and come out at the last moment to jump on board the coach. That's the way the Professor would do it, if he knew that someone might be watching for him with a cocked six-gun.

Nobody else seemed to be buying tickets. Twenty minutes later, the Professor heard the stage coming. He stood and drifted across the street. More than a dozen people gathered as the stage arrived. It was still a big deal to see a stage race into town. A lot of people met the afternoon train the same way. It was a link with civilization.

On the same side of the street as the depot now, the Professor could see the bench. The people there stayed where they were. Six people got off the stage, claimed their baggage and spread out into the town. The three people waiting to board were still there.

As the curious faded away, the Professor moved closer and studied the menu on the window of the café next to the depot. He'd eaten there once and had not been impressed.

Turning to the man on the bench again he wondered if he could be Mace Duncan. The Professor shook his head and concluded that it didn't seem likely. Poorly dressed at best, clean shaven, and wearing horn-rimmed spectacles, the man on the bench was everything Mace Duncan was not.

Ten minutes later, the driver came out and waved the people aboard. The man on the bench climbed the step first and eased down into the far window seat. The two women followed. The Professor kept watching the depot, but no one else bought a ticket. He stared into the café and even went inside the doors. No one at all was in the café that time of day.

The Professor stepped back to the street just as the stage pulled away. So that was that. Just where had Duncan hidden and how was he planning to leave town?

The Professor strode quickly down the

street to the livery stable. The man on duty shook his head at the Professor's questions. No tall bearded man had rented a horse that morning or afternoon, nor a carriage or buggy.

"We don't rent a lot of horses anymore," the man said. "The train has hurt our business a lot. Maybe if the town grows some we'll do better. Last year we had a much better year."

The Professor thanked him and walked slowly down Main. He was at the hotel when he saw Eagle coming. He shrugged in reply to Eagle's questions about Duncan. Then he asked Eagle what he had found at Duncan's house.

"Looks like he left for sure," Eagle said. "There are things missing. One curious thing I noticed was that below the mirror there are hair clippings and some shaving soap all over the place. Looks to me like Duncan might have shaved off his beard."

The Professor cried in surprise. "I've been watching him for a half hour, but figured he wasn't Duncan. He was clean-shaven with horn-rimmed glasses. He was one of the passengers on the stage to California. Come on, we have to rent horses and chase the stage!"

Chapter Sixteen

It took 20 minutes for the Professor and Eagle to get to the livery stable, pick out two horses, saddle them, and get away from town.

"How much of a lead do they have on us?" Eagle asked.

"The stage pulled out at four on the button. Now it's a minute to five. In these hills we should be able to make up an hour before dark."

"Maybe," Eagle said. "If they get to their relay station for fresh horses before we catch them, we're in trouble."

They rode hard, working the mounts on a fast canter for half a mile, then walking for half a mile, then cantering again. After an hour, they lifted the canter to a two-mile stretch, and the animals reacted well.

"I figure we're making a good six miles an hour," Eagle said. "The stages can't average that in these hills. Every steep grade cuts them to a slow walk."

They rode harder. Once they thought they caught a glimpse of the stage far ahead down a long slope, but they weren't sure. Another mile on they met a lone horseman riding the trail.

"How far ahead is the stage?" the Professor asked.

"A mile and a half, maybe two miles. They just left the swing station with I met them."

The Professor thanked him and he and Eagle rode harder. They galloped their mounts for a quarter of a mile, then walked them for a quarter of a mile before galloping again. Although both horses held their own, Eagle's mount was the stronger.

"Go ahead, try to stop the stage," the Professor said when he saw he was falling behind. "I'll be along as fast as this one can make it. If you get there alone, don't bother trying to capture that killer alive. Just be careful. There are two innocent women on board."

A half hour later, Eagle turned and couldn't see the Professor behind him. He kept the animal on the gallop-and-walk sequence, and the big mare held up well. On the next gallop, he came through some trees and ahead on a slight down slope he saw the stage. The horses were walking, and the driver riding the brake hard to keep the rig under control.

The rig was only a third of a mile ahead. Eagle kicked his mount and surged forward. One more walk and on the next gallop he came around a bend in the wagon trail and saw the stage 100 yards ahead.

"Yah," Eagle shouted: When he kicked the mare, she sprinted ahead. He saw a man on top of the rig turn and look at him, and Eagle held up one hand, hoping the people on the stage would understand he wasn't going to rob them.

The stage slowed to allow Eagle to catch up with it. When he did, he rode alongside. The driver was holding a shotgun, but didn't point it at Eagle.

"Hello, there. I'm a special deputy sheriff from Prescott. We've got a report that you've got a killer on your stage. I want to have a talk with the gent."

The driver looked at him with curiosity. "Special Deputy, huh. More like a highwayman. Where's the rest of your robber crew?" He swung the shotgun up to cover Eagle.

"No robbery. We want the man you have inside the coach, the older-looking, clean-shaven gent."

The driver looked at Eagle confused. "You chased us out here just to talk to the man," the driver asked.

"Talk to him and take him back to trial. If he's ready to surrender."

A shot blasted from the inside of the coach, and Eagle grabbed his left arm, but the bullet only creased him. To protect himself, Eagle shied his mount out of range behind the horses.

"That should be proof enough of who he is. Now can I get down and go reason with the madman?"

"Hell, yes! Why didn't you say so." The driver swung the shotgun around to cover one of the stage doors. Eagle was on the same side. The coach moved as if someone got in or out.

"The other side!" Eagle bellowed and kicked his horse around the lead team toward the far side. All he saw was a pair of dark pants sliding into the deep woods along the trail. Ponderosa pines and a lot of Douglas fir trees rose high over their heads. The territory got enough rain here so considerable undergrowth and brush covered the area.

Eagle guessed that the shot that creased him could have been from a derringer. The Professor hadn't said anything about seeing a six-gun on the man waiting for the stage. Eagle dropped from his horse and darted toward the brush. A second shot blasted from the dark green, but it missed, and a moment later, Eagle dove into the brush and lay still.

When he could hear movement ahead of him, he lifted and moved cautiously, not making a sound. Relying on his early Indian training, he penetrated the brush and tall trees without a whisper. The sound of Duncan moving ahead stopped. Eagle remained still.

Ten seconds later the sound ahead started but this time it was a panic-filled run as Duncan raced away without bothering to hide his movement. Eagle knew that meant he had an open place, or he had reloaded his derringer and wanted a closer shot.

Eagle listened another few seconds. Duncan was moving in a wide arc. Eagle cut across the arc, moving quickly, silently. With any luck he would intercept Duncan before the murderer could realize Eagle was there.

The sound of Duncan's running stopped again, and Eagle froze to the ground where he knelt. When the sound started, the man seemed to move in the same direction. He probably thought he was running straight ahead. Eagle drew and cocked his six-gun, holding it low as he ran in a crouch toward a three-foot-thick ponderosa pine tree ahead, which was where Eagle figured he and Duncan should meet.

Eagle looked around the big pine and heard the noise before he saw brush move. Then a man came through the tangle and stopped to pick up his fallen hat before he hurried on. He was clean-shaven and wore old clothes, and a hat that covered most of his face. He wasn't wearing his glasses now.

Eagle let him get within 15 feet of the pine tree before he stepped out and lifted the Colt. "Mr. Duncan, it's the end of the line, right here."

Duncan gasped, then exploded in anger and fear. He scratched for the derringer and charged straight ahead.

Eagle shot him in the right thigh and he went down. Even though Duncan was in pain, he pulled out the derringer as he lay on his back. He rolled and fired, but the round missed its target. Eagle shot him in the right shoulder and jolted the small pistol from Duncan's right hand.

"Bastard!" Duncan howled. "You're not a deputy sheriff. What business is it of yours to mix in this?"

"I'm helping out a friend. You want to forget that little shooter, or you want me to splatter your brains all over these woods?"

Duncan ignored the derringer and looked up. "Hell, you're a damn Indian."

"And you're a damned white-eye. My bullet doesn't care what color your skin is; it kills any man just as dead. So, do you want to get up and walk back to the stage road, or do you want to meet your maker right here and now?"

Slowly, Duncan stood and faced Eagle.

"You looked better with the beard," Eagle said. "It hid your natural ugliness. Now march back the way you came. You know you were running in a circle?"

They were almost to the edge of the trail through the woods when Duncan held a heavy branch and then let it snap back against Eagle. It jolted his weapon from his right hand, and before Eagle could recover, Duncan ran again.

Eagle ignored the weapon he had dropped and darted forward. He caught up with the fleeing man and drove into Duncan's back with his shoulder, smashing him to the ground. Then Eagle lay across Duncan's back, caught one of his arms, and twisted it upward on his back until he heard the small bone in the arm crack.

Duncan bellowed in pain.

Five minutes later, Eagle had collected his Colt and pushed Duncan out to the stage road. The stage had waited about a quarter of a mile down the road. The driver brought the rig up, and the Professor came behind, leading Eagle's horse.

The Professor scowled. "Didn't think we were going to have trouble capturing this bastard."

"Neither did I," Eagle said.

They got Duncan's suitcase off the stage and then waved good-bye to the driver. It was dusk by that time, but there was enough light for the Professor and Eagle to see as they went through the suitcase. It held no money, no stocks and bonds, no jewels. Eagle came up to Duncan from behind and began patting his pockets. He produced the stacks of $100 bills. He took one from each coat pocket and another one from each of Duncan's front pants pockets. They both stared at Duncan.

"How much did you steal from Mrs. Johnson?" the Professor asked. Duncan only shook his head. Eagle drove the side of his hand hard into the side of Duncan's neck, and he screeched in pain and dropped to his knees.

"Two more like that and I'll break your

neck and you'll be dead in five minutes," Eagle said softly.

"Christ, who are you guys? All right, all right. I have a little over fifty thousand dollars left. It's all there."

"Better damn well be," the Professor said. "I'd have rather that you tried to escape, Duncan. Come on, give it a try, you might make it."

Duncan looked at him, pointed to the bloody wound on his leg. "Not until you bandage my leg and my shoulder and put a splint on my arm. Damn Indian broke my arm!"

"Lucky it wasn't your head he broke. We'll wrap you up so you don't bleed to death. Take off that jacket and your shirt so we can tear it into bandages. Then we'll see if the county has any courts set up yet."

After they bandaged him and made a sling for his arm, the Professor put a rope around Duncan's neck and made him walk the two miles to the swing station. The head wrangler there loaned them a horse to get Duncan back to town.

It was past nine o'clock when they got to Flagstaff. A tall man with a white hat and a tin star on his chest met them.

"Deputy Sheriff Conswell from Prescott," he said to the three men. "Hear you

230

went after a man who's committed a couple of murders."

"True, Deputy. We had to take him off the afternoon stage to California. He didn't want to come back."

"We heard of the three killings. We have a warrant and complaint, and the trial starts first thing in the morning on the Ross Franklin killing. If we need to after that, we'll move on to the deaths of the other two men."

The Professor and Eagle turned the prisoner over to the deputy, who had commandeered a windowless storehouse behind the blacksmith to serve as the jail. Then the Professor and Eagle went to see Mrs. Johnson. She stared in disbelief when Eagle took the money out of his big pockets.

"Supposed to be a little over fifty thousand dollars there, Mrs. Johnson," the Professor said. "Duncan admitted he stole it, and right now a deputy sheriff from Prescott has Duncan in his newly made jail. Duncan's trial starts tomorrow morning on murder charges for the death of Ross Franklin."

"I'm glad about the trial. But all that money. It's mine?" Mrs. Johnson was totally surprised.

"Absolutely," Eagle said. "He stole it.

We found it on him when we took him off the stage. It's all yours."

Tears formed in her eyes and she brushed them aside. "I just don't know what to say."

The trial, the next morning, lasted three hours in the Logger's Rest Saloon. The judge from Prescott had come up with the sheriff's deputy and the district attorney. A local lawyer defended Duncan, but his heart wasn't in it.

The jury of 12 men came back with a guilty verdict after a half hour of deliberation. In the cause of justice, the judge pronounced the sentence of hanging, and set the time for 5 p.m. that same day.

There was little time to gather a crowd, but more than 200 people witnessed the carrying out of the sentence, including Mrs. Johnson and the widow Maria Escobar. Juan Romero stood close to Maria and had to steady the lady when the trap dropped.

Early the next morning, the Professor and Mrs. Johnson paid a call on banker H. L. Rushmore.

"Mr. Rushmore, when the word gets out about Mr. Payne and how he helped cheat Mrs. Johnson," the Professor said, "your bank is going to be a shell of a business. No one will trust you or anyone you employ."

"Mrs. Johnson has a business proposition for you. We know that last year your profit for the bank was a little over three thousand dollars. Your bank building is worth about a thousand. Mrs. Johnson is prepared to give you two years profit plus the cost of the building, and she'll buy out your bank and all of its current depositors, loans and transactions, for the sum of seven thousand dollars."

They watched Rushmore a moment and saw that he was shivering. "You'd let the story out and ruin me?"

"We have every responsibility to the public to let them know how your bank cheated me, Mr. Rushmore," Mrs. Johnson said. "If you're no longer in business here, the story need not be made public. That would mean you could start a banking firm in some other city."

A half hour later, Mrs. Johnson's attorney had the signed papers, and she owned the bank.

Thinking to help Juan get a good job, the Professor told Mrs. Johnson how good he was with figures, and how he had recovered and returned to the people of two villages almost $20,000. "Juan would make a fine bank president and operating officer for you. There are some things he would need to learn, but he's a quick young man."

Mrs. Johnson smiled. "And our money would be safe."

"I think the men in our group would consider transferring our money from San Francisco here for Juan to watch over for us. That's another 325,000 dollars."

"Rushmore has agreed to stay on for two months to get the new bank president and his new teller established," Mrs. Johnson said. "Now all we have to do it talk Juan into doing it."

Juan resisted for about ten minutes. Then he asked the question they had waited to hear. "Can we transfer the Willy Boy Gang money here from San Francisco?" Juan was hooked into the job and they all grinned.

Mrs. Johnson had a celebration dinner for them at the three story mansion that evening. Maria was there in a pretty new dress, and Effy came on Gunner's arm wearing her best dress and glowing like a bride.

Juan hovered around Maria as if she might suddenly vanish on him. The Professor bit off the end of a cigar and lit it, smiling at everyone. Willy Boy came wearing two guns and looking glum because the Professor had told him absolutely that he couldn't bring his regular whore from the saloon to the dinner. Eagle arrived late with ink smudges on his hands. He'd worked all the previous night and all that day on his Comanche ceremonies book.

Willy Boy lifted a glass of wine and stood. "I propose a toast to the last meeting of the Willy Boy Gang. We've done what had to be done, and we saved our necks. Each of us had a shot at righting some wrong or searching for someone. We've written the last chapter, as our writer friend, Eagle, would put it. Hell, I've learned a lot.

"I hear we're leaving two of our members here in Flagstaff and that Juan is becoming a hotshot banker. He's had a lot of experience in banks, but mostly it's been from the other side of the cage."

They all laughed and Juan grinned.

"But now he's off on a new life, and I envy him. Me? Well, I figure to head back to the rails to get to Missouri. Once there I'll do some scouting around to try to pick up the trail of the man who gunned down my pa. I figure without a bunch of baggage holding me down, I'll be able to run him to ground this time."

The other men in the gang hooted at him and he grinned.

"Yeah, well, maybe I can run him down even without the help of the rest of you. That's about it for me. We blasted out of that jail in Texas and saved our necks, and now we're ready to move on to another phase of our lives. Don't know what I'll do after I find Conover, but you can bet that I won't be in the banking business." They laughed again. "I mean from either side of the teller's cage." Willy Boy lifted his glass again, then sat down.

The Professor was next. He stood and looked at each of the men around the table.

"I don't know what I would have done without you guys. I'd probably be in prison now or dead in some unmarked grave. You brought me through. I got my heart's desire in Denver and I appreciate it. I think I've about burned that out of my soul."

"You remember that little lady I knew in Denver? From what I heard last, she was heading for Cleveland. Her name is Elena Griffin, and we exposed her father's theft back in Cleveland. Now I'm going to try to find her. If I do, I just might settle down back east there somewhere."

Willy Boy laughed and shook his head. "Not a chance."

The Professor grinned. "You're right. What I'm thinking of doing now is setting myself up in the detective business. I might even change my name and work for Pinkerton for a while to learn the rest of the techniques and tricks of the trade. Yes, I think that's what I'll try."

Eagle looked around and saw the other men watching him. He stood with practiced ease and smiled at them all. "I figure you know what I'm going to do. I haven't made it any secret. I'm going back to Denver, where I'll continue writing on my books on the Comanches. After this book on ceremonies, I'll want to go live with some of my Comanche cousins in Texas for a while. I'll be gathering material for my books if I do. Living with them will be a great opportunity to take notes and make drawings.

"I want to preserve for posterity the culture and the life style of the Comanche people. Within a hundred years all of the pure Comanches will be gone, and I don't want my culture and the Comanche way of living to be lost forever.

"My librarian friend in Denver suggested ten books on the Comanche. That may be too many, but I can see at least eight. That's about it. When you come through Denver, stop by at the public library and ask for me. I'll be around there close somewhere."

Juan, who sat beside Maria, stood stiffly. "I'm not used to making speeches," he said.

"Hell, a banker's got to talk a lot," Willy Boy said.

Juan grinned. "I guess. I'm scared of this new job. I've never been in a bank I wasn't robbing before." They laughed. "So now I have to learn all about banking. I figure I can do it, and I promise I'll protect our money and Mrs. Johnson's and whatever other money's there. At least I'm going to try."

He sat down. Maria's hand crept over to his and held it below the table, where no one could see. She smiled at him and nodded.

The rest of the people at the table looked at Gunner. He didn't bother to stand. First he grinned, then he laughed. "You know I'm gonna stay here and help out at the mill, and Effy and me are getting married." He was finished with his speech, and everyone cheered.

The dinner and the party lasted into the small hours of the morning. Eagle, Willy Boy, and the Professor would all take the morning train east. About one o'clock in the morning, the five men got together and all shook hands one last time.

They were free men, they were on their own, the gang was no more, but somehow it felt right. Each one had his own special place in life now, a direction, a purpose. The Willy Boy Gang would fade into the history of the violent West, but the five remaining members would go on and live their lives as they had to.

Willy Boy summed it up as tears slipped down his cheeks there in the Johnson mansion: "It was a rough go for a while, but as it turned out, the Willy Boy Gang had a damn fine ride!"